Of all the mishaps that had happened today—stubborn cattle, broken gates, his quad running out of gas—Wyatt Black definitely hadn't seen this one coming.

His boots scuffed in the dust leading to the sagging porch; his gaze riveted on the oddly shaped lump next to his front door. It was rounded and…pink. Pink? After a pause, he quickened his steps. A sound came from the bundle—a small squeaking sound.

Three steps later his heart pounded as his eyes confirmed his initial assessment. It was, indeed, a baby seat. For a few brief moments he'd nearly convinced himself he was seeing things. But there was no mistaking the pink canopy. Two steps away from the seat he could see a tiny white chubby hand, the fingers curled in, delicate pink fingernails tipping the tiny digits.

And then there she was. A tiny mite of a thing, eyes closed and lips sucking gently in and out with her breath as her hands moved restlessly. A hint of dark fuzz peeked out from beneath a stretchy pink hat, and a blanket patterned with white and pink teddy bears covered all of her but her hands. *A baby.* And beside her a navy and white cloth bag, as if announcing she was staying for a while.

Dear Reader

As a writer, I'm often asked, 'Why romance?' It's an easy question for me to answer. Romance is about hope. Not just a happily-ever-after, but the hope that there is someone out there to love us, and accept us, and face the ups and downs with us. It's the hope that even after we've faced challenges life can be good again. Not just good—even better than ever before.

Hope. It is, I think, the most optimistic word in the English language.

If anyone is in need of hope, I think it is Elli. Life has dealt her a rough hand, and she's taken some time away to regroup. Wyatt, too, hasn't had it easy. And when they first meet they don't exactly hit it off. But then something happens. Maybe it's a miracle. Because somehow a tiny baby enters the picture and she changes everything. Baby Darcy might bring a whole lot of trouble, but she also brings something to Wyatt and Elli that is desperately needed: hope.

Why romance? Because in my heart I believe in love, and healing, and happiness. I wish that for you, too.

Happy reading!

Donna

Next month, look out for
A BRIDE FOR ROCKING H RANCH by Donna,
in the magical collection
Christmas Wishes and Mistletoe Kisses

PROUD RANCHER, PRECIOUS BUNDLE

BY
DONNA ALWARD

MILLS
BOON

First published in Great Britain 2010
Harlequin Mills & Boon Limited,
Eton House, 18-24 Paradise Road, Richmond, Surrey TW9 1SR

© Donna Alward 2010

ISBN: 978 0 263 21438 3

Harlequin Mills & Boon policy is to use papers that are natural, renewable and recyclable products and made from wood grown in sustainable forests. The logging and manufacturing process conform to the legal environmental regulations of the country of origin.

Printed and bound in Great Britain
by CPI Antony Rowe, Chippenham, Wiltshire

A busy wife and mother of three (two daughters and the family dog), **Donna Alward** believes hers is the best job in the world: a combination of stay-at-home mum and romance novelist. An avid reader since childhood, Donna always made up her own stories. She completed her Arts Degree in English Literature in 1994, but it wasn't until 2001 that she penned her first full-length novel and found herself hooked on writing romance. In 2006 she sold her first manuscript, and now writes warm, emotional stories for Harlequin Mills & Boon's Romance line.

In her new home office in Nova Scotia, Donna loves being back on the east coast of Canada after nearly twelve years in Alberta, where her career began, writing about cowboys and the west. Donna's debut Romance, HIRED BY THE COWBOY, was awarded the Booksellers Best Award in 2008 for Best Traditional Romance.

With the Atlantic Ocean only minutes from her doorstep, Donna has found a fresh take on life and promises even more great romances in the near future!

Donna loves to hear from readers. You can contact her through her website at www.donnaalward.com, visit her myspace page at www.myspace.com/dalward, or through her publisher.

To my girly girls, Ash and Kate.
Love you.

CHAPTER ONE

OF ALL THE MISHAPS that had happened today—stubborn cattle, broken gates, his ATV running out of gas—Wyatt Black definitely hadn't seen this one coming.

His boots scuffed in the dust leading to the sagging porch, his gaze riveted on the oddly shaped lump next to his front door. It was rounded and...pink. Pink? After a pause, he quickened his steps. A sound came from the bundle, a small squeaking sound.

Three steps later his heart pounded as his eyes confirmed his initial assessment. It was, indeed, a baby seat. For a few brief moments he'd nearly convinced himself he was seeing things. But there was no mistaking the pink canopy. He took the veranda steps slowly, confused. What the hell?

Two steps away from the seat he could see a small white chubby hand, the fingers curled in, delicate pink fingernails tipping the tiny digits.

And then there she was. A small mite of a thing, eyes closed and lips sucking gently in and out with her breath as her hands moved restlessly. A hint of dark fuzz peeked out from beneath a stretchy pink hat, and a blanket patterned with white and pink teddy bears covered all of her but her hands. *A baby.* And beside her a navy-and-white cloth bag, as if announcing she was staying for a while.

Wyatt's heart raced as the necessary questions flew through his mind. He put down his toolbox with a quiet thud. Who was this child's mother and, more importantly, where was she? Why had a baby been left on *his* doorstep?

It was inconceivable that this miniature human could be meant for him. There had to be some mistake. The alternative was momentarily staggering. Was it possible that she might be his flesh and blood? He stared at the lashes lying on her china-doll cheeks. She was so little. He counted back several months, then breathed out in relief. No, it was impossible. A year ago he'd been outside Rocky Mountain House working as a roughneck. There'd been no one. He had always kept his relationships on the unserious side and short. There'd been no sense letting a woman get her hopes up when he hadn't been in a position to settle down. He wasn't into playing games.

He exhaled fully. No, this baby wasn't his—he was sure of it. The core of tension in his body eased slightly, but not completely. The baby couldn't be his, but that still left the question—*whose was she?*

And what was he supposed to do with her?

As if hearing his question, she lifted her fringe of black lashes and he caught sight of dark eyes. The hands waved even more as she woke. Then, as if knowing he was the last person she should see, her face scrunched up pitifully and a thin cry pierced the silence.

He breathed a profanity in shock and dismay. He couldn't just leave her there crying, for God's sake! What should he do now? He knew nothing about babies. He glanced around the yard and up the road, knowing it was a futile exercise. Whoever had left her on his doorstep was long gone.

He reached out and grasped the white plastic handle of the car seat, picking it up with his right hand and tugging open the front door with his left. He certainly had to get the baby out of the September chill—surely it couldn't be good for her. He didn't even stop to take off his boots, just went straight through to the kitchen at the rear of the house and put the seat on a worn countertop. The thin cry echoed—seeming sharper, stronger in the confined space. Wyatt took off his hat and hooked it over the knob of a kitchen chair before turning back to the unhappy bundle.

He lifted the blanket, momentarily marveling that a creature so tiny and fragile could emit such a shrill, ear-piercing cry. A quick search of the recesses of the seat revealed no clues to her identity, and he ran a hand through his hair as the cries increased, feet wiggling furiously now as well as hands.

"Shhh, baby," he murmured, his stomach sinking beneath the weight of the situation. He couldn't just leave her this way. He reached out to unfasten the buckle strapping her in and pulled back once he caught a glimpse of his hands. He'd been herding stubborn cattle and fixing run-down fences all morning. Pulse still hammering, he rushed to the sink and the bar of soap he kept on the rim in an old chipped dish.

He scrubbed his hands in the water, all the while looking over his shoulder at the baby, his nerves fraying as the cries grew more impatient. Instinct told him that he should pick her up. Babies needed to be soothed, right? After all, he'd be pretty ticked off at being strapped into a seat all day. He threw the hand towel next to the sink and went back to the seat. "Shhh," he repeated, desperate now to stop the crying. "I've got you. Just stop crying."

He released the strap and reached out, took the baby, blanket and all, from the seat and rested her on the crook of his arm.

The red blotchy face signaled more crying, and the wee body stiffened with outrage.

"Hey," Wyatt cajoled, wondering now if he shouldn't call 911. Surely this was an emergency. How many people came home to find a baby on their doorstep, after all?

How had this possibly happened?

Dimly he recalled that a bag had been on the veranda along with the seat. It was his best hope for a clue, he realized, so, baby and all, he opened the sagging screen door with his hip and retrieved the bag. His boots thunked on the scarred hardwood as he went back to the kitchen and the counter, putting the bag on top. Trying to ignore the crying, he wrestled the zipper with one hand while holding the baby tightly with his other arm. Perhaps in here there would be a name, an address. Some way to sort out this horrible mistake and return the baby to where she really belonged.

He pulled out a handful of tiny diapers, then a pair of pajamas with soft feet, and a stuffed animal. One, two, three bottles…and a can of some sort of powder added to the collection on the counter. Then more bottles. He ran his hand along the inside of the bag. More clothes, but nothing else.

Irritation flared, now that the initial shock was fading away. This was craziness, pure and simple. For God's sake, what kind of person left a baby on a stranger's porch and walked away? What kind of mother would do such a thing? What if he hadn't come back for lunch and she'd been left there all day? He let out a frustrated breath. Okay. Without a doubt the smart thing to do would be to call the police.

And then he felt it. Something stiff near the front of the bag. He lifted a Velcro tab and reached into a front pocket. An envelope.

Adjusting the baby's weight on his arm, he opened the flap, went to a kitchen chair and sat down. Heavily.

His eyes scanned the page. As if sensing something important were occurring, the infant quieted and she plunged a fist into her mouth, sucking noisily and whimpering. Wyatt read the brief words, his back sagging into the chair, staring at the plain paper and then at the tiny girl in his hands.

Holy jumpin' Judas.

Her name was Darcy. He said her name, tried it out on his tongue, his throat closing as the sound of his voice faded away in the quiet kitchen. The answer that greeted him was a fresh wail punctuated by a sad hiccup.

The break had helped only to increase the baby's vocal reserves. Her crying rose to a fever pitch and Wyatt closed his eyes, still reeling from the contents of the letter. He had to make her stop so he could think what to do next. His stomach rumbled loudly, reminding him why he'd come back to the house in the first place.

Maybe *she* was hungry, too.

As the inspiration struck he grabbed one of the bottles off the counter where he'd unloaded the diaper bag. At the first touch of plastic nipple to lips, Darcy opened her mouth and frantically started sucking at the milk inside. That was it! A sense of pride and relief raced through him as he went to the living room, sitting on the old couch with its sagging cushions and wiggling arms. He leaned back, rested his feet on a wood box he had pressed into use as a coffee table. Blessed silence filled the room as she drained the small bottle, her tiny body nestled into the crook of his elbow. She felt foreign there, unlike anything he'd ever held before. Not unpleasant. Just…different.

Her eyes drifted closed once more. Had he actually put her to sleep, as well? Thank God. With some peace and quiet, he could take a look at that letter again, try to sort it out. One thing was for sure...Darcy—whoever she was—couldn't stay here.

The little lips slackened and a dribble of milk slid down her chin into the soft skin of her neck. He was struck by how tiny, how helpless she was. As gently as he possibly could, he slid her back into her seat and covered her with the blanket. Then he went to the fridge, got out an apple to substitute for the lunch he'd missed. He took a bite and returned to the letter he'd left open on the table.

He read it again, and again, and once more for good measure. Half his brain told him there was some mistake. The other half, the part that nagged and taunted him each day of his life, nudged him cruelly and said he shouldn't be surprised. The apple tasted dry and mealy in his mouth, and he swallowed with difficulty.

Darcy was his niece.

Born to a sister he'd pretended hadn't existed.

He rubbed a hand over his face. Oh, he'd known for a long time that his father wouldn't win any awards for parent of the year. But he recognized the name at the bottom of the plain sheet. Barbara Paulsen had been two years behind him in high school. All the kids had known that she had no dad. She'd borne her share of ridicule, all right. *Bastard Barb,* they'd called her. He cringed, thinking about the cruelty of it now. He'd never joined in the teasing. It would have been too easy for the tables to be turned. He'd deserved the name as much as she had. There'd been rumors back then, of his father having an affair with Barb's mother. Barbara's dark hair and eyes had been so similar to his—and to Mitch Black's.

He'd always hated that he'd favored his father rather than his mother in looks. He didn't want to be *anything* like his father. Ever.

He'd chosen to turn a deaf ear to the rumors, but inside, a small part of him had always taunted that it was true.

According to the letter, they shared the same father. It wasn't much of a stretch for Wyatt to believe her. It had been no secret in his house that Mitch Black had married Wyatt's mother to do the right thing after getting her in trouble. And it had been a disaster.

Wyatt scowled, staring at the wall behind the table. Hell, even dead, his father still created ripples of destruction. Now Barbara—claiming to be his sister—found herself in the same position, and was asking for his help. Temporarily. But asking for it just the same.

The fact that she had left Darcy on his step meant one of two things. Either she was as great a parent as their father had been, or she was desperate. Reading between the lines of the letter, he was leaning toward desperation.

But it didn't solve a damn thing where he was concerned. He was now in possession of an infant. And he was a single man, trying to run a ranch, who knew nothing about babies. Maybe he should simply call the authorities.

He ran a hand over his face, heaving a sigh. The authorities, though, would call child welfare. He knew that much. And if Barbara were truly his half sister, she'd already suffered enough. He'd made no contact with her since leaving Red Deer. It had been easier to pretend she didn't exist. Easier to ignore yet another symbol of the disrespect Mitch had shown his family.

No, if he called, Family Services would take the baby away. Not just from him, but maybe from her, too, and the thought made his stomach clench.

Once he made the call, there would be no taking it back. What he needed to do was buy some time. He needed to talk to Barbara. Figure out the whole situation and make a better decision.

An ear-splitting scream shattered the air, scattering his thoughts into tiny fragments and making his eyes widen with the sheer panic echoing in his ears. He looked over— Darcy's face was red and the cries had a new, desperate edge to them. What now? He walked the floor, holding Darcy in the crook of his arm, at his wit's end. Until today, he'd never held a baby in his life.

He needed help. Even to make it through this one day so he could figure out what to do next. Maybe he shouldn't, but he felt responsible. Even if it turned out not to be true, he felt an obligation to make the right decision. It wasn't Darcy's fault she'd been left here. If what Barbara Paulsen said was true, she was family.

You shouldn't turn your back on family. He'd always believed it somehow, but had never had the chance to prove it.

His muscles tensed at the persistent wails. He couldn't do this, not alone. Who could he possibly call? His parents had been gone nearly five years. He'd been in the house only for the summer, after drifting around the upper half of Alberta for years now, earning his fortune in the oil patch and never staying in one place for long. He was alone, and for the most part that was how he liked it.

Until now. Right now he could really use a helping hand.

And then he remembered his neighbor. Not technically his neighbor either. He'd met Ellison Marchuk exactly once. She was housesitting for the Camerons, and despite being incredibly attractive, had no more sense than God gave a flea. Whatever possessed a woman to go traipsing through a pasture housing his bull—in search of flowers!—was beyond him. And then she'd had the nerve to call him grouchy, with a toss of her summer-blond hair. Grouchy as a wounded bear, if memory served correctly.

Ellison Marchuk would not have been his first choice, but she was a woman and she was next door, both qualifications that put her head and shoulders above anyone else he knew. Surely she would have some idea what to do with a baby. At this point, looking at the tiny face twisted in agony, *anyone* would know what to do better than he did. His nerves were fraying more by the minute. He just needed help quieting her crying. He'd take it from there.

Amidst the shrieking cries and against his better judgment, he wrapped the blanket around Darcy and headed for the door.

Elli rubbed her eyes and slid a bookmark into the textbook, pushing it to the side. If she read any more today about profit-and-loss statements she'd go cross-eyed by the end of the week. Taking the courses by correspondence had benefits and drawbacks. Still, they'd help her get back on her feet, something she needed to do sooner rather than later. Being laid off from the hospital was just the icing on the cake after the year from hell. It was time to take action. To find a purpose again.

Right now she just wanted a cup of hot chocolate and something to break up her day—make her stop thinking. She'd had way too much time to think lately. About all her failures, mostly.

She jumped as someone pounded on the front door, and she pressed a hand to her heart. She still wasn't used to the way things echoed around the vaulted ceilings of the Camerons' house, including the sound of her footsteps as she went to the foyer. The house was so different from the condo she'd shared with Tim in Calgary. It had been nice, in a good area of town, but this was...

She sighed. This was exactly what Tim had aspired to.

This was the sort of McMansion he'd mapped out for them. Maybe he'd get it yet. Just not with her.

The pounding sounded again. She peered through the judas hole and her mouth dropped open. It was the neighbor, the new rancher who lived next door. Her teeth clenched as she recalled their one and only meeting. Wyatt Black, he'd informed her in a tone that could only be considered brusque at best. He'd yelled at her and called her stupid. The remark had cut her deeply. Normally she would have brushed off the insult—she'd been called so many names as a clerk in the emergency room that she'd developed a thick skin. But in light of recent events, it had made her eyes burn with humiliation. She'd called him something, too, but she couldn't remember what. She vaguely remembered it had been more polite than the words going through her mind at the time. She'd stomped back to the house and hadn't seen him since.

Now here he was, all six brawny feet of him. Elli pressed her eye up to the peephole once more and bit down on her lip. Dark hair and stormy eyes and a mouth pulled tight in a scowl. And in his arms…

Dear Lord. A baby.

As he knocked on the door again, Elli jumped back. Now she could hear the thin cries threading through the solid oak. She reached out and turned the heavy knob, pulling the door inward, and stepped out into the afternoon sun.

"Oh, thank God."

Elli's eardrums received the full blast of the infant's cries mediated only by Wyatt's deep but stressed, voice.

"What on earth?"

Mr. Dark and Scowly stepped forward, enough that his body started to invade her space, and she stepped back in reflex.

"Please, just tell me what to do. She won't stop crying."

Whatever Elli's questions, they fled as she looked from his harried expression down into the scrunched, unhappy face. First things first. Her heart gave a painful twist at the sight of the baby. He clearly expected her to know what to do. She hated how her hands shook as she reached out for the soft bundle. The little girl was clearly in discomfort of some kind. And this rancher—Black—was certainly not calming her in the least.

Elli pushed the door open farther with her hip, inviting him in as she moved aside, trying to ignore her body's response to feeling the small, warm body in her arms. This baby was not William. She could do this. She pasted on an artificial smile. "What's her name?"

He swallowed thickly as he stepped over the threshold, his Adam's apple bobbing. Elli's gaze locked on it for a moment before looking up into his face. He had the most extraordinary lips, the bottom one deliciously full above a chin rough with a hint of stubble. The lips moved as she watched. "Darcy. Her name is Darcy."

Elli felt the warm little bundle in her arms, the weight foreign, painful, yet somehow very right. She pressed a hand to the tiny forehead, feeling for fever. "She's not warm. Do you think she's ill?"

Black came in, shutting the door behind him, and Elli felt nerves swim around in her stomach. He was not a pleasant man. And yet there was something in his eyes. It looked like worry, and it helped ameliorate her misgivings.

"I was hoping you could tell me. One minute she was asleep, the next she was screaming like a banshee." He raised his voice a bit to be heard over the screaming racket.

Her, tell him? She knew next to nothing about babies,

and the very reminder of the fact hurt, cutting deep into her bones. She scoured her mind for the things she'd learned about soothing babies from the books she'd bought and the prenatal classes she'd attended. Food seemed the most obvious. "Did you try feeding her?"

"She seemed to be fine after I gave her the bottle from the bag," he explained, rubbing a hand over his hair. "She drank the whole thing, sucked it right down."

Elli wrinkled her brow, trying to recall if Sarah Cameron had mentioned that their reticent neighbor had a child. She didn't think so. He certainly didn't act like a man who'd come into contact with babies before. He was staring at her and Darcy with his eyes full of concern—and panic.

A detail pierced her memory, a remnant of classes taken what seemed like a lifetime ago. "Did you heat the milk?"

The full lips dropped open slightly and his cheekbones flattened. "I was supposed to heat it?"

Elli's shoulders relaxed and she let out a small chuckle, relieved. Immediately she lifted the baby to her shoulder and began rubbing her back with firm circles. "She's probably got cramps," she said above the pitiful crying. It seemed the easiest solution at the moment. She began patting Darcy's back. Hungry, gas, cramps. Elementary. At least she could fake knowing what she was doing.

"I didn't know," he replied, a light blush infusing his cheeks beneath the stubble. "I don't know *anything* about babies."

"You might as well take off your boots and come in for a minute," Elli replied, not wanting to admit that she knew little more than he did and determined to bluff her way through it. She knew she'd made a mistake going into his bull pasture earlier this summer and she already knew what he thought of her common sense. She'd be damned if she'd let him see a weakness again.

They couldn't stand in the foyer forever. An enormous burp echoed straight up to the rafters and a laugh bubbled up and out of Elli's lips at the violence of the sound coming from such a tiny package. She was pleased at having discovered the cause and solution quite by accident. The expression on Black's face conveyed such abject surprise that she giggled again.

"I'm Ellison Marchuk," she introduced herself, her shoulder growing warm from the soft breath of the baby as she sighed against her sweater. "I don't think we met properly last time."

"I remember," he replied, and Elli felt the heat of a blush creep up her neck straight to her ears. "Wyatt Black, in case you forgot," he continued pointedly. "Thank you. My ears are still ringing. I was at my wit's end."

Elli ignored the subtle dig. Of course she remembered meeting him. It wasn't every day a perfect stranger yelled at her and called her names. She was more polite than that, and had been making an attempt to start fresh. She lifted her chin. "You're welcome, Wyatt Black."

Goodness, Elli thought as the name rolled off her tongue. The name matched him perfectly. She watched with her pulse drumming rapidly as he pushed off his boots with his toes. Even in his stocking feet, he topped her by a good four inches. His shoulders were inordinately broad in a worn flannel shirt. And his jeans were faded in all the right places.

She swallowed. She needed to get out more. Maybe she'd been hiding out in the Camerons' house a little too long, if she was reacting to the irascible next-door neighbor in such a way. Especially a neighbor with rotten manners.

Elli led the way through the foyer into the living room,

determined to be gracious. The room faced the backyard, then south over the wide pasture where Wyatt's herd now grazed—the very pasture where she'd indulged herself in picking late-summer wildflowers in an attempt to cheer herself up. The fields here were huge. She'd had no idea she was in the same pasture as one of his bulls.

"The Camerons have a nice place." His voice came from behind her. "I haven't been inside before."

"My father used to work for Cameron Energy," Elli remarked. "The Camerons are like second parents to me."

Wyatt remained silent behind her and Elli added lack of conversational skills to his repertoire of faults.

She took him straight to the conversation pit with its plush furniture. Windows filled the wall behind them, flooding the room with light, while French doors led out to a large deck. She gestured toward a chair, inviting him to sit. "Would you like her back now? She seems much more contented."

She held out her arms with Darcy now blinking innocently, her dark eyes focused on nothing in particular.

"She looks happy where she is," Wyatt replied, looking away.

Elli took a step back and went to the sofa. She sat down and put Darcy gently beside her. He couldn't know how caring for a child—even in such a minor way—hurt her. She worked hard to push away the bitterness. If things had gone right, she would have been in her own home cradling her own son right now. She blinked a couple of times and forced the thoughts aside. It could not be changed.

"Won't she fall off?" Wyatt's hard voice interrupted.

The rough question diverted her from overthinking. She didn't know. How old were babies when they could start rolling over? She didn't want him to see her indecision, and she adjusted the baby on the sofa so she was lying safely, perpendicular to the edge of the couch.

"How old is she?" Elli guessed at a month, maybe six weeks. She still held that newborn daintiness. A precious little bundle who had been through what appeared to be a rough day if the mottled, puffy cheeks were any indication. Could a day with Wyatt Black be described in any other way? Elli ran a finger down the middle of the sleepers, smiling softly as the little feet kicked with pleasure. At least she'd elicited a positive response rather than more crying.

When Wyatt didn't answer her question, though, she looked back at him again. He was watching her speculatively, his eyes slightly narrowed as if he were trying to read her thoughts. She was glad he couldn't. There were some things she didn't want anyone to know.

"What do you do, Ellison?"

Ah, he hadn't wanted to answer her question, and she didn't want to answer his either. It wasn't a simple question, not to her. Answering required a lengthy explanation, and it would only add fuel to his comment in the pasture that day, when he'd called her stupid. Maybe she was. A fool, certainly.

Maybe it was time he left. There was something not quite right in the way he'd avoided her question, something that didn't add up. He could mind his own business and she could mind hers and they'd both be happy.

"She seems fine now, but perhaps tired. You should take her home and put her to bed."

Wyatt looked away. Elli's misgivings grew. Her heart picked up a quick rhythm again. The only information he'd offered was that her name was Darcy, and it wasn't as if the baby could dispute it. He didn't answer how old she was, he didn't know to heat a bottle... What was this man doing with an infant? Was the child his? And if so, shouldn't he know *something* about caring for her?

She braved a look. As much as she didn't want to get involved, she could still smell the baby-powder scent on her shoulder, feel the warmth of the little body pressed against her like a wish come true. She took a breath. "She's not yours, is she?"

His eyes captured hers, honest but betraying no other emotion. "No."

"Then whose…"

"It's complicated."

She put her hands primly on her knees to keep from fidgeting. She briefly thought of all the news stories about noncustodial kidnappings. Sure, he was a crusty, grouchy thing, but was he capable of *that?* She didn't want to believe it. "I don't feel reassured, Mr. Black."

His steady gaze made her want to squirm, and she fought against the feeling. Should she be frightened? Perhaps. But she hadn't put herself in the middle of the situation. He had. A man with something to hide wouldn't have done that, would he? "You don't know what to do with babies," she remarked, screwing up her courage. "You don't even know how old she is."

"No, I don't. I've never held a baby in my life before today. Does that make you feel better?"

There was a little edge of danger to him that was exciting even as warning bells started clanging. "Not exactly."

She had to be crazy. Despite their first meeting, Wyatt Black was a stranger with a strange baby, in a situation she didn't understand and she was alone in the house in the middle of nowhere. Calling the police had crossed her mind more than once. But then she remembered the look on his face as he'd handed Darcy to her. It wasn't just panic. It was concern. And while he said little, there was something about him that she trusted. She couldn't explain why. It was just a feeling.

She'd learned to trust her gut feelings. Even when it hurt.

She picked Darcy up off the sofa cushion, swaddling her in the blanket. She simply had to know more to be sure. To know that the baby would be safe and cared for. "I need you to explain."

"Darcy is my niece. I think."

The ambiguous response made her wrinkle her nose in confusion. "Mr. Black…"

He stood up from his chair, his long, hard length taking a handful of steps until he paused before her, making her crane her neck to see his face. His jaw was set and his eyes glittered darkly, but there was a hint of something there that elicited her empathy. A glimmer of pain, perhaps, and vulnerability.

He reached behind him into his back pocket and withdrew an envelope.

He held it out to her.

"Read it," he commanded. "Then you'll know just as much as I do."

CHAPTER TWO

ELLI STARED AT THE piece of paper, all the while aware of Wyatt standing before her, the faded denim of his jeans constantly in her line of vision. She read the letter aloud, her soft voice echoing through the empty room. Listening to the words made it more real somehow. Wyatt seemed to look everywhere but at the baby.

"'Dear Wyatt, I know right now you're probably wondering what on earth is going on. And believe me—if I had another choice...'"

Elli risked a glance up. Wyatt was staring at a spot past her shoulder, his jaw tightly clenched, his gaze revealing nothing. She looked back down at the plain piece of paper, torn from a notebook, with the edges rough and careless. Her stomach began an uneasy turning. This wasn't stationery chosen for such an important letter. This was hurried. Impulsive.

"I don't know if you were ever aware, Wyatt, but we share a father. I am your half sister. I tried to hate you for it, but you were never mean to me like the others. Maybe you knew back then. Either way... you're all the family I've got now. You and Darcy. And I'm not good for either one of you. If there were

any other way...but I can't do this. Take good care
of her for me."

The letter was signed simply "Barbara Paulsen."
If the letter were genuine—and she was inclined to think
it was—then he was telling the truth. Darcy was his niece.
More importantly, the words themselves disturbed her.
Twice she had said she had no choice...why?

"Your sister..." she began quietly.

His boots did an about-face and she looked up from
the paper. He was no longer directly in front of her. He
had moved and stopped at the front window, looking out
over the hedge and small garden. There was a stiffness in
his posture that caused Elli a moment of pause. Surely a
mother's care was better than this detachment. Faced with
an infant, Wyatt showed the same cold, stubborn side as he
had the afternoon they'd first met. Babies needed more than
bottles and a place to sleep. They needed love. She wondered if Wyatt Black was even capable of tenderness.

She cleared her throat. "Your sister," she continued, her
voice slightly stronger, "must trust you very much."

"My sister?" The words came out in a harsh laugh. "We
have a biological relationship, if that. I went to school with
her, that's all."

"You don't believe her?"

He turned slowly from the window. His dark eyes were
shuttered, his expression utterly closed, and she couldn't
begin to imagine what he was thinking. Nothing about his
face gave her a clue. She wanted to go over and shake him,
get some sense of what was going through his mind. It was
clear to her that there was a plea in Barbara's note. She
was asking for help. And he was standing here like some
judgmental god doling out doubt and condemnation.

"There were rumors...I ignored them. It certainly makes

sense—most of it anyway. It's not much of a stretch to think that my father…"

There, there it was. The flash of vulnerability, in his eyes and flickering through his voice. Gone just as quickly as it had surfaced, but she'd caught it. What sort of life had he had as a boy? He wasn't shocked at the discovery of his father's betrayal, she realized. But he was bitter. She had to tread carefully. She folded up the letter neatly and handed it back to him.

"What if it's not true?"

His lips became a harsh, thin line. "It probably is," he admitted. "But I need to find out for sure. In the meantime…"

"Yes," she agreed quietly, knowing he had to see that Darcy was his first priority. "In the meantime, you have a more immediate problem. You have Darcy. What are you going to do?"

"I am hopeless with babies. I know nothing about them." His dark eyes met hers, looking as if he expected agreement.

"That goes without saying," she replied, crossing her arms. "But it doesn't change that Darcy has been left in your care."

"I don't know what to do. A few hours and I've already screwed up. I've never been around babies."

Elli offered a small indulgent smile. At least he seemed concerned about getting things right. Maybe she was judging him too harshly. "You were one, you know. A baby. Once."

"My memory is a bit dim," he reminded her, but she could see her light teasing had done its work. His facial muscles relaxed slightly and she thought there might actually be a hint of a smile just tugging at the corner of his lips. Just as soon as it came, it disappeared, so that she wondered if she had imagined it. The moment drew out and Elli's gaze remained riveted on his face. When he wasn't looking so severe, he was really quite...

Quite good-looking.

Darcy kicked on the sofa, a tiny sigh and gurgle breaking the silence. Elli looked away, wondering what on earth the child might be thinking, totally oblivious to the chaos around her. She thought briefly of Darcy's mother, Barbara, and felt a flash of animosity. How could a mother, any mother, simply drive away and leave this beautiful child on a stranger's doorstep? Did she not know how lucky she was? And yet...there was a sense of desperation between the lines of her letter. For some reason Barbara didn't think she could look after her own daughter. She was so afraid that she'd left her on the front porch of a man little more than a stranger.

Wyatt sat down on the sofa on the other side of Darcy, the cushions sinking beneath his weight. "I know," he said, as if replying to the question she hadn't asked. "I don't know how she could do it either. I haven't seen her in years. Maybe it is all made up. But maybe it's not. And I can't take that chance with Darcy."

"What do you mean?" Elli turned to face him, keeping her hands busy by playing with Darcy's feet, tapping them together lightly. She was already feeling the beginnings of resentment toward a woman she had never met. Darcy was so small, so precious. Elli had learned from years working in the emergency room that she shouldn't judge. But it was different when faced with an innocent, beautiful child. She *was* judging. It was impossible not to. She would give anything to be playing with her own child's feet at this moment. She knew in her heart that if William had lived, nothing could have pried her away from him.

Wyatt scowled slightly, resting his elbows on his knees.

"If she is my niece, I can't just call the police, can I? Because we both know what will happen to her then."

Elli nodded, pulled out of her dark thoughts. She had to look away from Wyatt's face. Was that tenderness she'd glimpsed in his eyes? The very emotion she'd doubted he possessed only moments ago? He might be inept, but he was trying to do the right thing.

"I can't just let her go into foster care. If I do, maybe there's a chance that her mother will never get her back. I can't let that happen. At least not until I know for sure. I need to find Barbara, talk to her."

Elli tried hard to fight away the surge of feeling expanding in her chest. She could already feel herself getting involved, getting sucked into a situation not of her making. Coming here, housesitting for the Camerons—that was supposed to be her way of taking a first step toward building a new life. Her chance to try again away from the drama and pitying looks. *Poor Elli. Bad luck comes in threes. Whatever will she do now?* She'd had enough of it.

A bachelor next-door neighbor with a baby wasn't exactly the type of special project she'd been looking for. She drew her attention back to the letter.

"This woman, this Barbara, even if she is your sister, Mr. Black, deliberately left a six-week-old baby on the doorstep of someone she barely knew with no guarantees that you would even be there." Elli fought to keep the anger, the frustration, the passion, for that matter, under control. This wasn't a subject she could be rational about. She knew it. It was the exact reason she should steer clear of the whole mess.

"Doesn't that tell you how desperate she is?"

Without warning, tears stung the backs of her eyes and she bit down on her lip. She got up from the sofa so that he couldn't see her face. So he couldn't see the grief that bubbled up.

She went to the kitchen, going instinctively for the kettle to give her hands something to do. Losing William had nearly destroyed her. It had certainly destroyed her marriage. And now that baby Darcy was quiet and content, the emergency was over. There was no way on God's green earth she was going to tell Wyatt Black—a man she'd just met—the sordid story of her disastrous pregnancy and resulting divorce.

She plugged in the kettle and took out a mug, hesitating with her hand on a second cup, trying to regain control. She should send him on his way. Remind him to warm up the bottles and wish him well.

He appeared in the doorway to the kitchen, filling the frame with his solid figure. She paused, the cup in her hand, looking up into his unsmiling face. He had Darcy on his arm in an awkward position.

Elli sighed, putting the mugs down on the counter. She'd taken the new-baby classes with Tim by her side. Back then it had been with dolls and smiles and laughter as the instructor showed them how to do even the simplest things. She'd blocked out those times from her mind deliberately, because they were so painful. But with Wyatt and Darcy only footsteps away, they came rushing back, bittersweet. She'd been excited to be pregnant, but also overwhelmed by the impending responsibility of caring for a baby. How must Wyatt be feeling, thrust into the situation with no preparation at all?

"Here. Let me show you." She went over to him and was careful to touch him as little as possible. Her fingers brushed the soft flannel of his shirt as she adjusted the pink bundle just the way she'd held the doll in classes. She forced the pain aside and focused on the task at hand.

Darcy looked up, eyes unfocused, seemingly unconcerned. Elli moved Wyatt's hand slightly. "You need to support her neck more," she said quietly, remembering what she'd read and heard. "Babies can't hold their heads up on their own at first. So when you pick her up or hold her, you need to make sure she has that support."

He cradled her close. "Maybe I should call someone. I really don't have a clue. She'd be better off with someone else, right? You said it yourself. I'm hopeless."

His eyes were dark and heavy with indecision, and shame crept through her. How could she have said such a thing, knowing how hurtful it could be? No matter how grumpy or grouchy he'd been, she could do better than throwing insults around. Elli could see that he was trying to do the right thing.

"No one was born knowing how to look after a baby, Mr. Black." She kept up the use of his formal name. The last thing she wanted was familiarity. It would be too easy to get involved. The instinct to protect herself fought with the need to help. "And if it's true, you're family. Doesn't that count for something?"

"More than you know," he replied, but there was no joy in the words. "Well, she's here now. I have a ranch to run. How can I possibly look after a child and do all that too?"

It did look as if he was beginning to think of the issue beyond *Could you get her to stop crying.* The kettle began to whistle and Elli swallowed thickly. "Do you want some tea?"

He shook his head. "No, thank you. I should get going, try to figure this out. First of all, I need to find Barbara."

"You seem to place a lot of importance on family, Mr. Black. That's to your credit."

His jaw tightened again, and Elli flushed slightly, not

knowing how what she'd intended as a compliment had managed to give offense.

"People tend to appreciate what's in short supply, Miss Marchuk."

He'd reverted to using Miss Marchuk now, too. The heat in her cheeks deepened and she turned away to pour the boiling water into her mug. His footsteps echoed away from the kitchen down to the foyer again, and she closed her eyes, breathing a sigh of relief.

She heard the door open and suddenly rushed from her spot, skidding down the hall in her sock feet, wanting to catch him before he left altogether. "Mr. Black!"

He paused at the door, Darcy now up on his shoulder and her blanket around her. A gust of wind came through the opening and ruffled his hair, leaving one piece standing up, giving her the urge to reach up and tuck it back into place.

"Yes?"

His one-word response brought her back to earth. She'd remembered something else, like a page torn from a book. "Heat the bottle in hot water. Then put a few drops of the formula on the underside of your wrist. When it's warm, but not hot, it's the right temperature."

For a few moments their gazes held, and something passed between them that was more than bottle-warming instructions. She didn't want to think about what it might be; even the internal suggestion of it hurt. She took a step back and lowered her gaze to the floor.

"Thank you," he murmured, and she didn't look up again until she heard the click of the door shutting her away from them both.

Elli struggled for the rest of the afternoon, all through her tea and while she made herself a grilled cheese and ham sandwich for supper. It was comfort food, and one she rarely allowed herself anymore. The months of criticism from Tim had caused her to burrow further into her grief. And like a nasty cycle, the further she withdrew, the more she had satisfied herself with food. His cutting remarks about her figure had been only one hurtful part of the disintegration of their marriage.

She put her plate into the dishwasher and cleaned the crumbs off the counter. The problem was, she couldn't get Wyatt and Darcy off her mind. Remembering how William had died made her want to run away from the situation as fast as her legs could carry her. And on the flip side was knowing that on the other side of the line of poplar trees, in a very modest bungalow, there was a rancher who knew even less than she did about babies. One who cared about what happened. At the same time she knew that Darcy would be the one to suffer while he tried to figure things out.

She swallowed, went to the windows overlooking the fields to the south. Wyatt's cattle roamed there, the red and white heads bobbing in the evening dusk, where she lost sight of them over a knoll. How was he managing now? Was Darcy crying, and was Wyatt trying to soothe her?

Elli wiped her fingertips over her cheeks, surprised and yet not surprised to find she was crying. She'd never even had the chance to hear William's cries. The absence of them had broken her heart cleanly in two. She got a tissue and dabbed the moisture away.

What would Wyatt do when he had to work? Had he managed to feed her properly? It wasn't fair to Darcy that Wyatt learned these things in trial by fire. And it was only Elli's stupid fear preventing her from helping. Shouldn't the welfare of the baby come before her own hang-ups?

She wiped her eyes once more, pity for the infant

swamping her. Shouldn't someone put that baby ahead of themselves?

Before she could reconsider, she grabbed her jacket from the coatrack and made the short trek across the grass to his house.

Wyatt paced the floor, Darcy on his shoulder, her damp lips pressed to his neck. His shoulders tensed as he thought about all he should have accomplished around the farm this afternoon. He'd managed to boot up the computer long enough to find Barbara in an Internet search, but when he called the number listed, there was no answer. He'd tried twice since, during moments when he'd thought Darcy was asleep.

She managed exactly seven minutes every time, before waking and crying. Crying that stopped the moment he put her on his shoulder and walked the floor. Which was great in the short term. But at some point he needed to eat. Sleep. Do chores.

More than once he'd felt his control slipping and wondered if he was more like his father than he'd thought. God, he didn't want to think so. From Wyatt's earliest memories, crying hadn't been tolerated. Mitch Black made sure of that. Wyatt wanted to think he had more self-control than his father. More compassion.

But baby Darcy was testing him.

He'd try Barbara's number once more. And then he'd call someone. He tried to ignore the end of the letter. The part where she apologized and said she trusted him. He'd given her no reason to. And yet…something about it made him feel as if he would be failing her if he didn't do this.

He sighed, turning back toward the kitchen, craning his neck at an odd angle to see if Darcy was asleep. It was almost as if he was operating on two levels—the one that needed information and planning, and the one with the immediate, pressing problem of keeping a baby's needs met.

Suddenly he had a new respect for mothers who seemed to juggle it all with aplomb.

A knock on the door broke the silence and Darcy's hands jerked out, startled. A quick check showed her tiny eyes open again. Wyatt pushed back annoyance and headed for the door, with a prayer that it was Barbara saying it had all been a mistake.

Instead he found Ellison Marchuk on his dilapidated porch.

"Oh," he said, and she frowned.

"Disappointed, I see." She pushed her hands into her jacket and he fought against the expansion in his chest at seeing her again.

This afternoon he'd been an idiot. He'd rushed over there thinking only of getting help, but he'd been inside all of thirty seconds when his priorities had shifted. He was supposed to have all his thoughts on his predicament, and instead he'd been noticing her hair, or the way her dark lashes brought out the blue in her eyes, or how her sweater accentuated her curves. He wasn't disappointed at all. Even though he should be.

"Not at all," he mumbled roughly. "I was just hoping it was Barbara, that's all."

"It would solve everything, wouldn't it?" She offered a small smile. His gaze dropped to her full mouth.

"Are you going to invite me in, Mr. Black?"

Of course. He was standing there like a dolt, thinking how pretty she looked in the puffy fleece jacket. Clearly she wasn't thinking along the same lines, as she persisted in calling him Mr. Black. Her body language this afternoon had spoken volumes. She couldn't even meet his gaze at the end, and she'd taken a step back.

And now here she was.

He moved aside and held the door open for her to enter.

Instantly his eyes saw his house the way hers must— in stark comparison to the pristine, high-class Cameron dwelling. They were from two different worlds. It couldn't be more plain from the look on her face.

"I haven't had time to pay much attention to the inside," he explained, then mentally kicked himself for apologizing. He didn't need to apologize, for Pete's sake! It was his house, purchased with his own money. He could do what he damned well pleased with it. He'd be a poor rancher if he put dressing up the inside ahead of his operation.

"I expect you've been busy," she replied softly.

"Something like that." He forced himself to look away, away from the brightness of her eyes that didn't dull even in the dim lamplight.

"I just wanted to see how you were making out with Darcy."

"I can put her down for exactly seven minutes. After that, she starts crying again." He shifted the slight weight on his arm once more. "So I keep picking her up."

Her gaze fell on his arms and desire kicked through his belly, unexpected and strong.

"Babies like to be snuggled," she murmured. "Think about it. If you had spent the first nine months of your life somewhere that was always warm and cozy, you'd want that on the outside, too."

Was it just him, or had her voice hitched a little at the end? He studied her face but saw nothing. He realized she was standing in front of the door with her coat and shoes on. He should invite her in. She'd helped once today. Perhaps she could again.

"I'm sorry, Miss Marchuk..." He paused, hearing how formal that sounded. "Ellison. Please...let me take your coat and come in. I managed to make coffee. I can offer you a cup."

She looked pleased then, and smiled. His heart gave a slight thump at the way it changed her face, erasing the seriousness and making her look almost girlish. She unzipped the fleece and put it in his free hand.

"Coffee sounds great," she replied. "And please...call me Elli. Ellison is what my mother calls me when she's unhappy with something I've done."

She looked so perfectly sweet with her blue eyes and shy smile that he answered without thinking. "You?"

She laughed, the sound light and more beautiful than anything he'd heard in a long time.

"Yes, me. Don't let the angelic looks fool you, Black."

He turned away, leading her to the kitchen while his lips hardened into a thin line. Angelic looks indeed. He'd been captivated by them twice today already. As he considered the bundle on his shoulder, he knew that one complication was enough. No good would come out of flirting with Elli Marchuk. He'd best remember that. His life was here, this house, this ranch. Anything else was transient, capable of moving in and out at a moment's notice. He'd built his life that way on purpose, one planned step at a time. The last thing he wanted was to be foolish and impulsive and end up as unhappy as his parents had been.

Being careful to support Darcy's head, he tried once more to put her into her seat. He'd only just retrieved mugs from the cupboard when she squawked again.

He sighed. There was a reason he'd never aspired to parenthood.

"Have you fed her?"

Elli's voice came from behind him. It sounded like a criticism and he bristled, knowing full well it was a legitimate question but feeling inept just the same.

"Yes, I fed her. She burped, too."

The squawking quieted as Elli picked her up, and Wyatt turned around, trying hard to ignore feelings of inadequacy as Darcy immediately stopped fussing.

"Maybe she's uncomfortable. What do you think, sweetheart?" Elli turned her conversation to the baby.

"What do you think is wrong?" Wyatt asked, putting the coffeepot back on the burner.

A strange look passed over Elli's face, one that looked like guilt and panic. But it was gone quickly. "I couldn't say," she replied.

"But you were so good with her this afternoon." Wyatt put his hands on his hips.

"Lucky, that's all. I just...remembered a few things." The same strange look flitted over her features once more.

Wyatt took the coffee to the table. "You fooled me. You looked like you knew exactly what you were doing." So much that Wyatt had felt completely inept. A feeling he despised. He was used to being the one in control.

Elli and Darcy walked the length of the kitchen and back. After a few moments she admitted, "I haven't really cared for a baby before. The things I thought of were simply things I'd heard about. Not from experience, Mr. Black."

Her chin jutted up, closing the subject but making him want to ask the questions now pulsing through his mind. But then he remembered the old saying, "Don't look a gift horse in the mouth." He'd benefit from whatever insight she had and be glad of it.

"I don't really know what babies need," he admitted. "I

fed her, patted her back like you did, walked her to sleep, but every time I put her down…"

Wyatt almost groaned. Of course. He'd forgotten one important thing. He'd been so focused on getting formula the right temperature that he'd forgotten to check her diaper. Not that he had any clue what to do there either.

Pulling calves and shoveling out stalls was far less intimidating than one tiny newborn.

"She's probably due for a diaper change, isn't she?" He tried to sound nonchalant. This was a perfect opportunity. Elli must know how to change a diaper. He could simply watch her so he'd know better for the next time.

Instead, Elli came around the corner of the counter and placed Darcy back in his arms. "Here you go, Uncle Wyatt," she said lightly. "You get diaper duty. I'll fix the coffee. Cream and sugar?"

Oh, boy, Wyatt thought, looking down into Darcy's pursed face, his smug plan blown to smithereens. He was in for it now.

CHAPTER THREE

WYATT HELD DARCY straight out in front of him. There'd been many firsts for him over the past few months, but this was something completely out of his league. For the first time in his life Wyatt Black was going to change a dirty diaper.

He glanced over at Elli, who was spooning sugar into cups without so much as a concerned glance in his direction. The last thing he wanted to do was look like a fool in front of her twice in one day. He did have a level of pride, after all. And he was generally a competent sort of guy.

But people—babies—were different than cows and horses and machinery. He wasn't nearly as sure of himself when it came to human beings. And not just babies. Each time he met Ellison, his tongue seemed to tie up in knots and nothing seemed to come out the way it should.

He went to the diaper bag, retrieved a diaper and laid the baby on her blanket. He removed her sleepers and some sort of snapped-on undershirt and then the diaper. Good Lord. Wyatt paused, unsure, completely out of his element. Darcy, who'd been sucking on two fingers, took the digits from her mouth and began to squall again, protesting against the cold. He heard Elli go to the fridge and back to the counter. He refused to look up to check if she was watching.

"Hang on, hang on," he muttered, trying to remember

how he'd taken the wet diaper off so he could put the new one on the same way.

"Do babies always cry so much?" he grumbled as he cleaned up Darcy. He reached inside the bag for a new diaper.

Elli came to his side, laying a hand on his arm. "It's the only way they have of saying what's wrong," she said quietly. His arm warmed beneath the touch of her fingers. It felt reassuring and friendly, not the kind of caress he was used to. The touches he was accustomed to were more demanding. Wanting something, rather than giving.

"Do you know how to do this?" he asked, holding up the tiny diaper.

"I haven't done it before…on a baby," she replied, her gaze darting away from his.

"Meaning you've done it *not* on a baby?" he teased, wondering what had put the dark look on her face.

"A doll," she replied, her lips firm. "I've diapered a doll before."

There was something in her voice that reached inside him and grabbed his attention. A defiance, and a defensiveness he hadn't expected. But did he want to know? No, he decided, he didn't want to dig into whatever reasons Ellison did or didn't have for anything. But it didn't mean he was insensitive to her feelings, whatever they were.

"Can we figure it out together?"

Her gaze went back to him now, the irises of her eyes a glowing sapphire. "Wyatt…"

She'd dropped the Mr. Black and used his first name. His gaze dropped to her lips—he couldn't help it. They were pink and finely shaped and very soft looking.

He had to be careful here. Very, very careful.

"Which bit goes at the back?" He shook the white diaper gently.

She pulled back a few inches and looked away. "I think this way," she said, sliding the diaper underneath Darcy's bum, tabs at the back. "And diaper cream. There should be some of that, right?"

Elli watched as Wyatt dug in the bag and pulled out a tube. When he handed it to her, their fingers brushed and she pulled her hand back quickly. The contact seemed to spiral straight to her tummy and she held her breath for a tiny instant.

"It doesn't bite," Wyatt quipped, and Elli forced a smile. Maybe it didn't, but she wasn't so sure about him. Unsure how to respond, she hesitated and looked at the label—it said barrier cream. Logically, it provided a barrier for the baby's tender skin. She smoothed some on with her fingertips, ignoring the odd sensation of knowing Wyatt was watching her.

"You don't want her getting a rash, right? And then..." She pulled the front up and went to fasten the tab. Only, she folded it over so it stuck to itself.

"Heck, I could have done that," he said from behind her, and she heard humor in his tone as her cheeks flamed. Darcy was looking up at her with wide eyes, as if to say, *Come on, people. What's the holdup?*

Elli began to laugh. Lordy, the situation was comical when she stopped to think about it. She heard Wyatt's warm chuckle behind her and then felt his body—*oh, God,* his very hard, warm body—pressed against hers as he reached around her to retrieve another diaper from the bag. "I hope we get it right this time," he murmured, his lips so close to her ear that she could feel the warmth of his breath. She suppressed a delicious shiver.

"We'd better. Or else you're going to run out of diapers in a hurry."

Elli slid the diaper under once more and this time

fastened the tabs securely to the waistband. "Ta da!" She slid away, needing to get away from him and his sexy voice and body. She avoided his gaze, the one she suspected was leveled right at her. Self-conscious, she tugged her thick sweater down over her hips, smoothing it with her palms. "Now you just have to get her dressed again."

She left him there and went to toss away the diaper and wash her hands.

He took out a new undershirt and pajamas and carefully dressed Darcy. Then he placed her in the seat and sighed, moving to tidy up the mess before taking his place at the table. After only a few hours, things that were not usually there were cluttering countertops. Bottles and creams and rattles, where there were normally gloves and keys and perhaps the odd tool. "I haven't had two moments to take a breath. And now I have to say thank you again."

"It was nothing," she replied quietly.

Wyatt's eyes narrowed. She had let down her guard for a moment, but there was something in her voice, something in the way she refused to meet his gaze right now. It had happened several times today. Evasion that told him there was a whole lot to Ellison Marchuk he didn't know. Whatever it was, it was her business. He took a sip of hot coffee.

The immediate issue was solved, but he was beginning to see there would be more. He had no proper baby equipment, a handful of diapers, a few more bottles left. He still had chores around the ranch to look after tonight— and more repairs in the days ahead than he could possibly imagine. Barbara had been a fool to leave her daughter here. Darcy belonged with her mother, not with him.

Elli watched Wyatt over the rim of her cup. She could almost see the wheels turning in his head as he mulled over what to do. She wondered if all that stuff ever erupted. She guessed it did. She suspected it might have been the case the day he'd read her the riot act in his pasture.

She was glad now that she'd followed her instinct and come over. Wyatt was trying to do the right thing, she could see that, but he was totally out of his depth. And he was proud. Watching him try to change the diaper had shown her that. He didn't want to ask for help. Men never did. And who would be the one to suffer? Darcy. Darcy couldn't explain to Wyatt that she was hungry or wet or uncomfortable or tired. Elli wasn't much more qualified. Everything she'd done today had been because of her pre-natal classes. She'd been so afraid of caring for William that she'd signed up for a baby-care course. Until today, she hadn't had a chance to put those classes to use.

Being with Darcy, feeling the tiny body in her arms, smelling the baby-powder scent of her was so bittersweet it cut deeply into her soul, but the alternative had been staying at home and wondering and worrying. What would Wyatt do with her during the day? There would be formula to mix, baths to give, diapers to change. How was he supposed to do that and maintain his ranch? He already looked exhausted.

Her gaze fell on the car seat, and the half-closed lids of the angel within it. Then back to Wyatt, his dark hair curling lightly over his forehead, his eyes dark with fatigue and worry.

"I can't thank you enough, Elli. Twice today I was at the end of my rope."

Elli knew that to get mixed up with the situation was a mistake. He just needed to focus on the good. "You're doing fine," she replied. "Not many men would have the patience to walk the floor with an infant."

"But that's just it." He ran his fingers through his hair.

"I'm not that patient. I…I don't want to lose patience with her."

He wouldn't, Elli was sure of it. Even this afternoon, when Darcy had been screaming incessantly, his expression had been one of utter concern and helplessness. She reached across the table and squeezed his arm. "I think you're just experiencing something every new parent does," she said. "You want to do everything right. I can see how you care for her already, Wyatt. You'll do what's best."

"I wish I had your confidence."

She smiled brightly, wanting to finish her coffee and get out of there. At the moment she didn't know which was more dangerous—Darcy and her baby-powder-scented sweetness or Wyatt's dark sexiness. "You'll be just fine."

She was just finishing the last swallow of coffee in her cup when Wyatt asked plainly, "What if you stayed to help?"

Her mug hit the table with a solid thunk. "What?"

"I know it's a huge imposition, but I need to find Barbara, and do chores, and I can't take her to the barn with me and I can't leave her alone in here. I'd like to hire you to help me."

Heat blossomed in her cheeks. Wyatt didn't strike her as the kind of man who liked admitting weakness. The very fact that he was asking meant he was admitting he was over his head. But she wasn't the solution. "I'm not sure I'm cut out to be a nanny for hire," she replied, hearing the strain behind her voice and knowing the source.

"Look, it'd only be temporary."

"I'm sure there must be services in town, or nearby. Someone more qualified." Caring for a baby full-time? Oh, she could just imagine what her friends and family would have to say about that. They might even be right.

"I can't run the place and watch her at the same time.

I need help. And if it's you…" He coughed. Looked over at the car seat. "The fewer people that know about this— at least for now—the better. I can't be sure someone else wouldn't make that phone call. I just want to keep her safe and do the right thing."

"You trust me, then?"

"Is there some reason I shouldn't?"

She shook her head. "No. I'm just surprised, that's all."

Wyatt took a sip of coffee. "At this point, you're in as much hot water as I am. You're an accessory."

The words came out as serious as a judge, but the tiny upward quirk of his lips was back. Was he teasing? He was, she was sure of it. Warmth seemed to spread through her as she realized it. Moreover, she *liked* it.

Elli didn't know if she should feel relieved or panic. Right now a little of both was running through her veins. This was all she'd ever wanted, in a sense. She'd never been keen on a career the way the other girls in school had been. She'd known all along she wanted to be a mother. To have a house full of children, a home.

She thought once more of her friends and family. They would remind her that this wasn't her home, and this wasn't her family. They would be right. But maybe it was high time she confronted all those hurts. And Wyatt…she could tell he was a proud man, but not too proud to put Darcy's needs ahead of his own. How could she say no to him when his motives were clearly honest?

She looked around her. Lord knew the house needed a feminine touch and it was a sad business, cooking for one. She should know.

"All right," she replied. Considering her unemployed status, she'd be foolish to turn him down. But only for a little while, until he could get things sorted out. She couldn't get attached. And it would be very easy to love the tiny pink slumbering bundle. Elli knew she could love Darcy without even trying. Yes, eyes wide open. That was how she had to look at it.

His breath came out in a rush. "Thank you," he said, his relief clear in each syllable. "You have no idea how grateful I am."

"We have two things to do, then," she said quietly. "First, Darcy needs things. Diapers, formula, clothing. Is this really all her mother left her with?"

Wyatt nodded.

Elli sighed. If she were going to tackle her fears head-on, she might as well tackle them all. Perhaps it was finally time to let go. There was a whole room in Calgary filled with unused baby items. Why was she keeping them? As a shrine to William? It made her sad thinking about it. If she lent them to Wyatt, at least they would be of practical use. She could make a quick trip to Calgary and pick them up, and simply tell him that she'd borrowed them from someone who didn't need them.

"If you're looking at short-term, I know where you could borrow some items. No need for you to buy things you may never use again. It does mean a trip to Calgary tomorrow…"

"I can watch Darcy while you go. I don't want to totally disrupt your life, Elli."

"Thank you, Wyatt." She was glad to be able to go alone. It saved a lot of explaining at both ends. If she didn't have Darcy with her, she could avoid the questions at her parents' house, the probing, motherly kind. And if Wyatt stayed here, she needn't explain why she was in possession of a complete layette.

"Perhaps you can get a lead on Barbara in the meantime."

"I agree," he said, rubbing his lower lip pensively with a finger. "I can't help feeling she's in some sort of trouble."

This wasn't quite as easily solved as baby amenities. Wyatt pushed away from the table and went to the sink, putting his cup within it and bracing his hands on the counter.

"I found her number, but she's not picking up. The address didn't have a street number. It appears to be a Red Deer number, though."

Red Deer. A spark of an idea lit, one that might be able to solve all their problems. Elli got up and retrieved the cordless phone from a dock. "May I? I might be able to find an address."

"By all means."

She dialed in a number, then pressed in more keys for an extension, hoping Joanne was working tonight.

She was, but the query came up empty. Elli hit the end key and thought for a moment.

"She didn't have the baby in Red Deer," Elli said, furrowing her brow. "If she had, there'd be a record of it at the hospital. Let's try Calgary."

"I thought they wouldn't give out patient information," Wyatt said, leaning back against the counter. He ran a hand through his hair, leaving the ends of the nearly black strands slightly mussed, and very, very sexy. Elli swallowed. She was tired, that was all, and the dark outside made the cozy kitchen seem more intimate than it truly was. She could still feel the shape of him pressed against her back earlier and tried to ignore her body's response at the memory.

"They're not supposed to." She hit the talk button on the cordless phone once more. "I used to work in the emergency department. I have friends who will do me a favor, that's all."

A smile creased his face and Elli's breath caught. It was a slow, devilish sort of smile that she hadn't seen up to this point. The kind of smile that could do strange and wonderful things to a woman's intentions.

"Are you breaking the rules, Ellison? Because I had you pegged as Miss Straight and Narrow."

The words stung even as she knew he was teasing. How often had she faced that criticism? His perusal of her sparked her self-conscious streak once more. Why couldn't she have hit the treadmill more often? She crossed an arm around her middle, attempting to hide the flaws he must see. "You wouldn't be far off," she murmured. "But that particular title isn't all it's cracked up to be."

"Your secret is safe with me."

The phone grew slippery in her hand as her nervousness went up a notch. She hadn't been this alone with a man since Tim. In fact, she'd gone to great lengths to avoid it. And now Wyatt was working some sort of spell around her.

She was here for Darcy, that was all. She was being neighborly. There were all sorts of reasons she should have accepted his offer, beyond her cash-flow problem. It was the right thing to do. She might not know exactly what she was doing, but so far she and Wyatt had stumbled their way through the day, hadn't they? Four hands were better than two, right?

"Do you want me to make the call or not?" A note of annoyance crept into her voice. Annoyance at him, and annoyance at herself for worrying so much what Wyatt Black thought. Her mother always said if there was a wounded bird around, Elli wanted to nurse it to health. It had always frustrated her, both the teasing and the criticism inherent in the words. Was it so very wrong? So many times she'd felt her choices were looked down upon simply because they didn't line up with others' expectations. "If you have a better idea…"

Wyatt's smile faded. "Make the call."

She dialed the number she knew by heart.

Five minutes later she hung up, the address jotted down on a notepad. "She had the baby in Calgary. I've got her address in Red Deer. Darcy is five weeks and three days old."

Wyatt's dark eyes met hers. "I think we should go by Barb's place before you go to Calgary, don't you?"

Elli nodded. "It doesn't make much sense to stock up on baby things if she's going to be going back home, right?"

But even as she said it, she got a heavy feeling in her stomach. Barbara wouldn't be there. Looking into Wyatt's face, she could see they both knew it. All tomorrow would be was confirming what they already guessed.

"There's something else," Elli said, putting the paper down on the counter. "She listed you as her next of kin."

Wyatt's mouth fell open and he pushed away from the cupboard. "She did?"

"Either she's telling the truth or she's planned this from the beginning. Somehow…"

"It doesn't make sense, right? If she weren't going to keep the baby, she would have come to me before. Or given it up for adoption."

His thinking was along the same line as hers. "I think so, too."

"Which means Darcy is, likely, truly my niece."

Elli fiddled with the pen. "How can you be so sure?"

Wyatt's brow wrinkled. "Without seeing Barbara, talking to her…I suppose I can't. We both know we're not expecting to find her tomorrow, are we? But Elli, I can't see her making all this up."

Elli couldn't either. Too many things fit together. "What

if she's simply gotten in over her head? She didn't mention the baby's father."

"I get the impression she's doing this alone," he replied, his voice sounding weary.

"Me, too."

"Then the best thing is to find her and talk to her, right?" Wyatt went to the fridge, avoiding her gaze. "Did you have dinner? I haven't eaten. I can make us a sandwich or…"

Wyatt stood, the fridge door open, a packet of roast beef in his hand. The whole conversation felt surreal to Elli. This morning she had been working on an accounting assignment. Tonight she was contemplating sandwiches with Wyatt Black and trying to help him figure out what to do with a baby.

He shut the door of the refrigerator, holding the meat, mustard, and a bag of lettuce. Elli eyed the roast beef, but declined once more as he held up his hand in invitation. She'd eaten already. And the last ten pounds she wanted to lose weren't going to fall off on their own.

"You haven't mentioned any other family."

"That's because there isn't any." He took a plate off a shelf and slapped two slices of bread on it.

"So if Barbara is your sister as she claims…" She let the thought hang.

"Then she's the only family I've got," Wyatt confirmed.

Elli thought about that for a moment. As much as her mother's meddling and worried phone calls drove her crazy, at least she wasn't alone. She knew she could go home and her mom would make her homemade cabbage rolls and perogies and her dad would convince her to stay to watch the hockey game. She couldn't imagine not having them there.

"Can I ask you a question, Elli?" Wyatt went about

building his sandwich, layering lettuce and meat on the bread.

"I guess." As long as it wasn't a question she didn't want to answer. There were lots of those.

"Why did you agree to help me?"

Ugh. She didn't want to answer, simply because there were so many possible responses. Granted, he'd barged into the Camerons' house today and demanded her help, but she'd come back tonight under her own power. It was a chance to feel as if it all hadn't been for nothing. All the hope and loss should have a purpose. Wouldn't this be a chance for something good to come out of all the bad?

And if they were going to care for Darcy, shouldn't she at least make an attempt at being friendly? Surely she could ignore the way her pulse seemed to leap when he was close and how her cheeks flushed when he touched her.

"Look," she said, "I'm going to be honest here. I'm housesitting for the Camerons because I'm at one of those places in my life. I lost my job in some recent streamlining and I..." She felt the words clog up her throat but forged on doggedly. "I got divorced not long ago as well, so I agreed to housesit to help make ends meet. I've been doing some courses online to upgrade my skill set. But for the most part I'm out here in the boonies with only myself for company and feeling fairly useless when all is said and done. When you came barging in today, I wanted to help. Because Darcy is innocent. And because at least I feel somewhat useful again. So you see, you're kind of getting me out of a jam, too."

Wyatt had stopped chewing and put down his sandwich during her speech. Now that it was over, he masked his surprise, finished chewing the bite that was in his mouth, and swallowed.

"I bet that felt good."

And his lips curved. His dark, scary scowls lost all their power when he smiled, replaced with something even more potent.

"It did. Maybe I danced around stuff far too long today. I don't make a habit of going around and spilling my life story." She found herself smiling hesitantly in return. As the seconds drew out she realized they were standing there grinning openly at each other, another notch in familiarity gained. She turned away, embarrassed, shoving her hands into her pockets. Wyatt Black could be darned alluring when he wanted to. And she'd bet he didn't even realize it.

"I'm sorry about your marriage."

His words were sincere, and she sighed. "Me, too. We shouldn't have married in the first place. We were very good at pretending we were what we wanted in each other. He's not a bad man, he just wasn't...the right man." Losing William had been the final blow to a marriage already failing. That was the true grief, the part she wouldn't share with Wyatt. Once William had died, there wasn't any point in keeping up the charade any longer.

"This isn't my usual method of meeting people either," Wyatt acknowledged. "In fact...I tend to keep to myself most of the time."

"I hadn't noticed," she returned, and then felt sorry she'd been sarcastic, even if it had been meant as teasing. It was a reaction to remembering their first meeting and the disapproval on his face as he had spoken so harshly to her. She hurried to cover the barb by turning the tables on him. "So...turnabout is fair play. Now it's your turn to tell me about yourself."

He considered for a moment. "I don't usually talk about myself."

"Me either, but I spilled. Now you owe me." She raised an eyebrow and let a teasing smile touch her lips.

The comfort level in the room rose. Now that Darcy was sleeping peacefully, some of the tension had dissolved and they were suddenly just a man and a woman. There were so many things she didn't know about him, like where he came from and why he'd bought this run-down farm in the first place. He was a big question mark. She'd spent these past weeks all alone. Despite their rocky beginning, he was turning out not to be a bad sort. It was nice to have someone to talk to who didn't know about her past, bringing her baggage to every single conversation. Someone who didn't think of her as *poor Elli*.

"The fact that I'm willing to believe that Barbara is my half sister tells you a bit about my home life, don't you think?"

"I take it your parents weren't divorced, then."

Wyatt shook his head. "Nope. If Barbara's my sister, then it's because my dad had an affair with her mother." As if he suddenly found the sandwich distasteful, he put the remainder on his plate and pushed it away. "I know Barbara's mother had a rough time making ends meet. You can bet that my dad didn't offer any support. If it's true he was her father, he left them high and dry. My dad—"

But then Wyatt broke off, took his plate to the garbage and dumped the sandwich into it.

"I'm sorry."

They were the only words Elli could think of to say. Anything else would sound trite and forced.

"Not your fault," he replied. "And none of it helps us now."

He moved as if to leave the room, but paused beside her, close enough that if he shifted another inch their sleeves would be touching. He smelled like coffee and fresh air and leather—a manly combination that had her senses swimming. Her breath caught simply at the powerful nearness of him.

"Nothing will change who my father was. He wasn't a very good man. Even if he isn't Barbara's father, I know he could have been."

Elli turned her head and looked at Darcy, sleeping so peacefully, and felt her heart give a painful lurch. Her mother and father had somehow found the magic formula. They'd always had a good, strong marriage. It was another reason her own failure cut so deeply. She turned her head back again and found herself staring at Wyatt's shoulder. Now here she was with Wyatt and his own dubious beginnings. Stuck in the middle of them both was Darcy.

"What about you, Wyatt?" She found she wanted to know, for Darcy's sake and for her own. She put her hand on his sleeve. "Are you a good man?"

His head tilted sharply downward as he looked at where her fingers met his arm. Then his eyes, nearly black in the dim kitchen light, rose again and captured hers. Her chest thumped again, but for an entirely different reason. There was something edgy and mysterious about him, all mixed up with a sense of unsuitableness. And the package was wrapped very nicely. Surly or smiling, Wyatt Black was unlike any other man she'd ever known.

"I doubt it," he replied. "I suspected the rumors about my father were true but never asked. I ignored it instead. What does that say about me? I stuck my head in the sand, just like my mother."

Her heart softened at his confession. "You're not like him, though," she said gently. "You're too good for that."

He pulled away from her grasp. "I wish I could be as sure of that as you."

CHAPTER FOUR

DARK CIRCLES SHADOWED Wyatt's eyes when he answered the door the next morning. He looked less than stellar, in faded jeans and a T-shirt that had seen better days. A suspicious spot darkened one shoulder. His hair was mussed on one side, as if he'd crawled out of bed only moments before. The thought made Elli's blood run a little bit warmer.

Elli stepped inside, out of the frosty chill. The mornings this week had been cool enough that she could see her breath in clouds. Wyatt's home, despite the run-down condition, was warm and cozy, and smelled deliciously of fresh coffee.

"Rough night?"

Wyatt raised an eyebrow, let out a small sigh. "Kind of. How did you know?"

She smiled, pointing at his shirt. "Spit up."

He angled his head to stare at the fabric. "I'm just tired enough to not be amused." Even as he said it, he offered a wry grin. "I didn't get more than a few hours. You?"

Elli hadn't slept much either. She'd lain awake a long time, wondering how he was faring with Darcy and if she had settled at all. When Elli had finally drifted into a fitful sleep, it had been to a mixture of dreams of Wyatt and William all jumbled up together. Her head kept drumming out a warning that getting involved was a grave mistake.

But her heart told another story, one of an innocent child caught in an impossible situation.

Personal wounds or not, it just wasn't in her to walk away and forget that someone needed her. Despite what she'd told Wyatt, this had nothing to do with the money. It had been so long since she'd been needed for anything—even if it meant learning as she went along.

"I worried about the two of you a little. How is Darcy now?"

"Napping."

She couldn't help the relief that flooded through her, knowing that things were going smoothly and there was no emergency that needed her attention. As much as she wanted to help, she wasn't very sure of herself. Laughing as she practiced diapering a plastic doll in baby-care class wasn't the same as caring for a live, breathing infant, not knowing how to soothe upsets or interpret crying. Yesterday she'd done a decent job of faking it. But the whole time she'd doubted herself.

They needed to find Darcy's mother and make things right again. She was skeptical they'd find Barbara at her home today. Elli held on to a little strand of hope that her intuition was wrong.

"You look like hell, Wyatt." She followed him into the kitchen, careful to step quietly in her stocking feet. "Did you get any rest at all?"

He shrugged and went for the coffeepot. "A little. Here and there. It was harder than I anticipated."

Elli hadn't expected him to admit such a thing. He seemed so proud and determined. Even yesterday he'd sought her help, but only when it clearly became too much for him to deal with. "Why don't you go sleep now? I'll stay and look after Darcy." The words came out far more confidently than she felt.

He handed her a cup and she heard him sigh once more. The thought had crossed her mind last night that she could stay at his house and give him a hand, as Darcy was sure to wake during the night. That's what babies did, right? Between the two of them surely they would have figured out what to do. But that also would have meant staying there, in his house, *with him.* Her visceral reaction to him last night had been unexpected. It had been attraction: elemental, surprising and strong. Staying overnight would not have been a good idea, and so in the twilight she'd made her way back over the dry grass to her house.

"I'm fine. I've gone on less sleep before, Elli. As soon as I've had something to eat, we can get going to Barbara's. The sooner we talk to her, the better."

"You don't want to go alone?"

"I was thinking that having Darcy with us might be a good idea."

Maybe Barbara would realize she'd made a mistake and Darcy would go back to her mother. Either way, surely Barbara would want to see her daughter and make sure she was okay.

While Elli sipped her coffee, Wyatt fixed himself some toast and spread it liberally with jam. He offered her the plate, almost as an afterthought, but she'd grabbed some yogurt and fruit already and waved him off. The quiet of the morning held a certain amount of intimacy. The past few months she'd spent utterly alone. To share coffee with someone over a breakfast table was a level of familiarity that seemed foreign. But surprisingly, not unwelcome. Perhaps she'd licked her wounds in private long enough.

Darcy was still sleeping when Wyatt came in from his chores, so Elli carefully fastened the safety buckles, getting her ready for the car. "We should put a blanket over her, right?" Wyatt looked up at Elli, waiting for confirmation.

Her heart thumped nervously. How could she explain her own trepidation and lack of experience without delving into a topic she had no wish to discuss? She couldn't, so instead of specific knowledge she relied on simple common sense.

"It is chilly this morning. A blanket is a good idea."

She was thinking about fastening the seat inside the vehicle when she remembered something else, a hang-on from her baby classes. "Babies should be in the backseat, Wyatt. But you just have your pickup, don't you?"

"Do you mean I can't take her in the truck?" He paused, hanging on to the car seat handle. He ran his spare hand through his hair.

"It has something to do with the airbags."

"I am so not cut out for this," Wyatt muttered. "I can't imagine what Barbara was thinking, leaving Darcy here."

Elli said nothing.

"Well? How am I going to put her into the truck?"

Elli's mouth opened and closed. "I don't know." She clenched her teeth, hating to admit she really didn't know.

"I thought women knew about these things."

Feelings of loss bubbled so closely to the surface that Elli grabbed his comment and answered sharply simply to cover. "That's a sexist comment if I ever heard one. And not the first time you've brought it up, by the way. I hate to disillusion you, Wyatt, but just because I was born female doesn't mean I'm hardwired to know a baby's needs."

"All the girls I knew in school babysat."

"You didn't know me in school." Her heart had started tripping over itself. She should have kept her mouth shut. Would he start asking questions now?

Would she answer him if he did? She bit down on her

tongue. No, she would not. She barely knew him. He didn't deserve to know about William. That was a treasure she held locked up, close to her heart.

His face blanked, his eyes and cheeks flattened with surprise. "I'm sorry. I guess I assumed all women want children. I didn't mean to touch a nerve."

And oh, that stung. It had nothing to do with wanting. No baby had ever been wanted more than her own. She blinked rapidly and turned away, opening the front door. "Wait here, and I'll get my car," she replied, knowing her tone was less than cordial but caring little. "We can take it instead." They would go and find Barbara, Darcy would go back to where she belonged and she could go back to ignoring Wyatt just as she had before.

On the walk to the Camerons' house, she felt her temper fizzle out, to be replaced by bleak acceptance. There was no sense questioning why she was helping Wyatt when on a personal level she didn't like him very much. It didn't matter that he seemed to rub her the wrong way or that she felt inept when caring for Darcy. It was quite simply that William was gone and his death had left a vast emptiness within her. But Darcy was not William, and Elli knew it quite well. It didn't stop the need to help. Or to hope that this would ease some of the grief she still felt whenever she thought of her son.

Back at Wyatt's, she helped him fasten the seat in the back, and spread a blanket over Darcy to keep her warm. She looked like a china doll, all pink and white, with delicate lashes lying on her cheeks as she slept. Wyatt paused for a moment, looking at Darcy, and Elli saw the hard angles of his face soften as he gazed down at her. When he caught her watching him, he turned away and got out of the back, shutting the rear door behind him. Elli, on the other side, touched the soft dark hair, wondering at the sheer circumstances that had landed her in the middle of such a situation. Wyatt was trying so hard. He could be irascible, but she also knew that he genuinely cared about Darcy already. He acted as if he was positive Darcy was his niece. And she'd seen the look in his eyes just now when he'd let down his guard. He would do the right thing by her.

The smart thing would be to resolve it as quickly as possible. To make things right and move on.

She motioned toward the driver's side. "Do you want to drive? You know where you're going."

At his brusque nod she handed him the keys. They'd check out Barbara's house first. And if they had no luck, they'd come back here and then she'd be off to Calgary. She could stop at her parents' house while her mom and dad were at work. She hadn't been able to bring herself to get rid of William's things before, but now was a good time. Someone should get some use out of them.

The drive to Red Deer was quiet, and when Wyatt pulled up outside a small bungalow, he got an eerie feeling. There was no car in the yard. The shades at the windows were all closed. No summer flowers bloomed outside like the surrounding yards.

Ellie stayed in the car while Wyatt got out, approached the front door. He knocked, rang the doorbell. No answer. Tried the doorknob; it was locked.

Getting back into the car, he sighed, then his lips formed a grim line. "No one's there. And I don't think anyone has been there for a while."

Ellie's face fell. "What about friends, other family?"

He shook his head. "None that I know of. I haven't been in contact with Barb for years."

What should he do now? The address was the only clue

he'd had. He couldn't even begin to know where to look, and he was still uneasy about bringing any authorities into it. He might not know much about babies, but the more he looked at Darcy the more he believed she was his niece. How could he do that to the only family he had in the world?

He couldn't. So it was up to him to come up with an idea.

"Wyatt, look." Elli pointed to the house next door. An older lady, slightly stooped and with tightly curled gray hair, had come outside. She paused when she saw the car, then picked up a watering can and moved to a tap on the side of the house.

"It's worth a try," he admitted, and got out of the car again.

"Morning," he called out.

The lady looked up, turned off the tap as Wyatt approached. "Good morning." She watched him with curious eyes.

"I'm looking for Barbara Paulsen. She lives here, right?"

"And you'd be?"

Wyatt swallowed. The answer had to be true and it had to put this woman at ease. She was looking at Wyatt quite suspiciously now, and he noticed her fingers tighten on the watering can.

"Family, but I haven't seen her in years. This is the last address I have for her, but nobody's home."

The answer seemed to appease the woman. "She lives here. We don't see much of her, though. She keeps to herself. Hardly ever see that baby she brought home. It's been a beautiful summer and last year she planted a whole bunch of petunias and marigolds. This year, nothing."

A huge lump of unease settled in Wyatt's stomach.

Dropping off a kid to a stranger, changes in behavior…he wasn't getting a good feeling.

"You don't know where she might be, do you?"

"Sorry." The lady put down her watering can. "I saw her leave yesterday morning, but I haven't seen her since. I can let her know you stopped in…"

She left the words hanging in the autumn air.

"Tell her Wyatt was here and I'd like to catch up with her." He aimed a smile in the woman's direction. At this point he felt he could do with any ally he could find.

"I'll do that."

Wyatt thanked her and went back to the car. No further ahead than before, except he now knew that she hadn't been back home since dropping Darcy off at his doorstep yesterday morning.

There was nothing to be done right now except go back to the ranch and try to come up with a plan on the way. Darcy's needs came first. He didn't want to have to go to the police, but if he kept coming up with dead ends, he'd have to.

He got into the car and shut the door, taking a moment to look back at the baby. "Darcy's still sleeping. Let's head home."

Elli nodded. "I'd like to get on the road. There are several things I can bring back that will make caring for her so much easier. A stroller, for one, so I can take her for walks, and something better than a car seat for her to sleep in."

He nodded and backed out of the driveway as Ellie's cell phone rang.

Wyatt kept his eyes on the road as Elli spoke on the phone. Seeing Elli this morning had made the day seem sunnier. For a small moment. Then he'd realized how stupid that was and he'd locked it down.

He passed a car and stared resolutely ahead. She looked so cute and cheerful, so sunny and blonde and...free. Just as she had that afternoon he'd encountered her in his pasture. He'd bet anything she was a real Pollyanna. She'd surprised him with her harsh words this morning, but he supposed he'd deserved it. He'd made a rash assumption, and he hated it when people did the same thing to him.

At least she'd walked away, so he hadn't felt the need to apologize.

Truth be told, he was glad for her help. Any attraction he'd felt last night in the intimacy of his kitchen was easy to tamp down. He wasn't interested. Certainly not in her. She had complication written all over her, and he avoided complications like the plague.

And the bit about his father...there could be no more of that. He'd felt an odd little lift in his heart when she'd expressed such confidence in his temperament. But she didn't know. She had no idea where he came from.

A snuffle sounded from the backseat and he glanced back. Darcy was still sleeping, the tiny lips sucking in and out. She was exhausted from her long night, just as he was. He wished he could catch up on his sleep as easily as she seemed to be able to.

A sigh slid past his lips as Elli chatted on the phone in the background. Like it or not, Darcy was his responsibility for now. If he wanted uncomplicated, he was in the wrong situation.

Elli's voice registered through his thoughts. "He's right here," she said. "Oh. *Oh.* I see. We'll be there soon."

Elli clicked her phone shut. "Wyatt, I have good news and bad news."

He looked over at her, unsettled by the anxiety that darkened the deep blue of her eyes. She bit down on her lip as he scowled back at her. Her teeth caught the soft pink flesh, and he had the momentary urge to kiss away the worry he saw there, to bring back the light, unfettered smile he remembered.

He pulled his attention back to the road. "Hit me."

"I know where Barbara is."

The flash of relief was quickly replaced by the knowledge that this was the good news and the bad news was yet to come; that it was likely about where Barbara was and he wasn't going to like it. "So? Where is she?"

"She was just admitted to the hospital." Elli tucked the phone back into her purse and straightened. "That was my friend—the one I called yesterday. She tried your number first, since you're next of kin. When she couldn't reach you, she took a chance and tried me."

Heaviness settled around his heart. Hospital? Was she sick? Barbara had trusted him because she was ill? How sick exactly? Scenarios ran through his head, none of them good. He kept thinking about her note and how she'd said she couldn't do it. A rock of worry settled at the bottom of his stomach. "Is she okay?"

"She was admitted to the psych ward."

Wyatt swerved and nearly put them off the road. "What?" His hands began to shake on the wheel and he pulled off onto the shoulder, putting the car in Park. Now he knew what had nagged him about Barbara when he'd read the note, the uneasy feeling he hadn't been able to put his finger on. Her mother had passed away when he'd been working in Fort St. John. The next time he was home and out having a beer with a few buddies, he'd heard the gossip about her death.

At the time he'd barely paid attention; small-town rumblings were really not his thing. But now he remembered, and the memory only added to his dread.

"Is. She. Okay." He ground out the words, fearful of the

answer, his mind on the innocent child in the backseat and what a huge dilemma this all was.

"Physically, you mean?"

He nodded, blocking out images that threatened to flood his brain. Awful possibilities. Scary ones.

Her hand came to rest on his forearm, lightly but reassuring. "Wyatt, what is it? You're white as a sheet."

Wyatt's muscles tensed beneath the weight of her fingers. Admitting to a complete stranger that he had a half sister in the world was bad enough. How could he explain to her that he already felt guilty about keeping quiet all these years? When they were kids, it was understandable. It would have caused trouble, trouble he tried to avoid at home. But once he was grown, he could have gone to Barbara and...who knows. He would have been away from his father's censorious anger and his mother's fearful glances. He might have had *family*.

Maybe that hadn't meant anything to his father, but it had meant something to him. When Barbara's mother had died, he'd let shame and embarrassment rule his good sense.

If he hadn't been so weak, maybe she wouldn't have been driven to what he suspected right now.

And he couldn't tell Elli any of it. He clenched his teeth. After all this time, it still ate at him.

"I just...the *psych ward*," he said meaningfully. "That's not good."

"You are listed as next of kin, remember. At least we know where she is now. They'd be contacting you regardless."

"They would?" He turned and studied her profile. Something was troubling her, more than the situation. He'd glimpsed it several times in the past twenty-four hours. As if she was remembering something unpleasant, and it was weighing her down. Much as he was feeling the deeper in he got.

She nodded, but wouldn't look at him. "Oh, yes. A new mom, showing up at the emergency room, needing a psych evaluation?" Finally she turned toward him, and her earnest gaze hit him like a punch in the gut.

"Don't you see? You can't protect her now. The first thing they are going to want to know is where her baby is."

CHAPTER FIVE

ELLI'S WORDS SANK IN, one heavy syllable at a time. Of course. He'd watched the news enough to know that a new mother coming into an emergency room without her baby would set off alarm bells. Added to that he really didn't know what sort of state Barb was in. All he could feel was the heavy weight of knowing that Darcy was relying on him completely.

"Then we have to go there, don't we." The situation had changed now and the weight of responsibility grew heavier on his shoulders. This was no longer a few days of child care—it was now complicated by bureaucracy. Everything would be recorded, noted, in some chart. He felt the walls closing in and hated it.

Elli nodded. "Yes. If we don't, like I said, you're listed as next of kin. You'll be the first place they look for Darcy anyway. And this way, Wyatt...well, it wouldn't hurt to have Darcy looked over, as well."

"Will they take her away?" He looked at Elli, needing her to say no. The very thought of losing Darcy now to complete strangers was incomprehensible. He might not have been prepared, but he was family. Surely that counted for something. He had Elli to help him. It disturbed him to realize how much he needed her.

Elli felt her heart leap at his question, not so much the

words but the way he said them—unsure, and slightly fear-ful. The man had been up most of the night; he had never looked after a baby before, by his own admission. But the concern, the fear she saw on his face now touched her, deep inside. She wished she could put her arms around him and tell him it would be fine. But what would he think of her if she did such a thing? He'd read more into it than she'd intend. And they had to keep their relationship—the completely platonic one—separate from Darcy.

There was more to Wyatt than she'd initially thought. He wanted to do right by this baby. How could she fault him for that?

She couldn't. She applauded him for it.

He checked his rearview mirror and then pulled a U-turn, heading back the way they'd just come, back to the highway. She had to answer him honestly. "I don't know, Wyatt. I'm not in social services, though I would think they would want her to stay with her family. Let's just take it a step at a time, okay?"

Wyatt nodded, but she saw the telltale tick in his jaw anyway. She reached over and patted his thigh, meaning to be friendly and supportive. Instead she was struck by the intimacy of the gesture, the warmth of his denim-clad leg beneath her fingers, the way the fabric wrinkled just so at the bend of his knee. The small touch made her feel a part of something, and that scared her. She pulled her hand away. "It'll all work out," she reassured him. It had to. If not for her, for them. She'd do whatever she could to make sure of it.

She was relieved they had found Barbara, but as they drove south Elli twisted her fingers. This wasn't how she'd planned on today playing out. The agenda hadn't included a visit to the hospital, faced with old coworkers and remind-ers. And now Wyatt would be with her when she went to pick up the baby things. How could she possibly explain why she had a roomful of newborn paraphernalia at her mother's? What if she broke down? She didn't want to cry in front of him.

She would get through it somehow, she promised herself as she stared out the window. She had come this far. She would fall apart later. After all, she'd spent months pretending and going through the motions in public. She only had to do it for one more day.

Once they were inside city limits it took just ten minutes to reach the hospital. They parked in the parkade and made their way through to the emergency department.

"I'll stay with Darcy," Elli suggested, taking the baby seat from his hand and adjusting the strap of the diaper bag on her shoulder. She needed space from him, space to think without him always so close by.

She wished that Barbara was anywhere but here, at the Peter Lougheed Hospital. Inside were her old coworkers, many who had been her friends but who had drifted away from her since William's death and her divorce from Tim. There had been so many awkward silences in recent months. But she lifted her chin. What did she have to hide? Nothing. Why shouldn't she face them? Their whispers didn't matter anymore. Steeling her spine, she gave the car seat a reassuring bounce, tightening her grip. It didn't matter, not anymore, and she was tired of running away.

"You go ahead and check with the triage nurse," she suggested to Wyatt. "I'll stay in the waiting room with Darcy. She's waking up and you need to find out what's going on."

Wyatt went to the triage line and spoke to a nurse while Elli sat in one of the padded vinyl seats. She undid the chest strap to Darcy's seat and lifted the baby out, cuddling her in the crook of her arm.

Oh, she felt so good and warm, smelling of powder and the scent that was distinctly *baby*. "Hello, sweetheart," she murmured softly, not wanting to be overheard by the others in the room. She fought away the insecurities that had plagued her on the drive and decided to enjoy whatever time she had with Darcy. Being with her made her feel better, not worse. "You were such a good girl in the car," she whispered, touching the tiny fingertips, looking into the dark blue eyes that stared back at her, slightly unfocused. The little fist moved and clasped her finger tightly.

And just like that, Elli lost her heart to the tiny girl in the pink blanket. She blinked several times and swallowed past the lump that had formed in her throat. "Your uncle Wyatt and I are going to do everything we can for you, little one. I promise."

It felt strange joining their names together that way, but Elli knew she meant it. She already cared about Darcy so much, and Wyatt couldn't do it alone. She just wouldn't deceive herself into thinking it was something more, no matter how much her senses kicked into overdrive when he was around. She wasn't interested in fairy tales. She was interested only in reclaiming her life.

Wyatt returned, his face looking pinched and his gaze dark with worry. "Her doctor wants to speak with us," he explained. "Both of us, and to see Darcy."

She nodded. "Yes, but she's going to be wanting a bottle soon."

Wyatt picked up the empty car seat. "Okay." His shoulders relaxed as he turned away. But then he turned back once more and reached down for her free hand.

His strong fingers gripped hers and her heart thumped in response.

"Thank you, Elli. For everything over the last twenty-four hours. It helps knowing that Darcy is being taken care of, that I…" He paused, and a slight tint of pink stained his cheeks. "That I don't have to do this alone. It means more than you know."

He spun back toward the sliding doors, which opened on his approach. Elli's jaw dropped a little as she followed him; he expressed more confidence in her than she had in herself. Taken care of? Elli was feeling her way through this as much as Wyatt. But she couldn't stop the glow that spread through her at his words. Her confidence had taken such a beating since William's death. There were times she felt she'd failed at everything—wife, mother, even her job. Wyatt Black—ornery, pigheaded cowboy—had offered more encouragement than anyone else had in the past months. Not just with Darcy, though that was part of it. When he looked at her, she almost felt pretty. Desirable. That was as much of a miracle as anything.

She gently touched Darcy's nose as she passed through the doors. "I'd better be careful, huh, little one?" she whispered. "Before long I'll start *liking* him, and then we'll really be in trouble."

They were shown not to a curtained exam room but a different room, one with four walls and a door that the nurse shut behind them. They waited only moments before the doctor came in and shut the door behind her.

"Mr. Black, I'm Dr. McKinnon." The young woman held out her hand and Wyatt shook it. "I'm the one who admitted Ms. Paulsen earlier this morning. We admitted her for postpartum depression, and we'll be meeting and assessing her over the next several days."

"I'm just glad she's all right," Wyatt replied, but Elli noticed his face was inscrutable. The emotion he'd shown her only moments ago was gone, and in its place a wariness she thought she might understand. This hospital had been her home away from home, yet she was no more looking forward to the questions she'd face today than Wyatt was. At least she had the choice not to answer. A month ago standing in this department would have filled her with dread. Today, with Wyatt beside her, it didn't matter quite as much.

Dr. McKinnon looked at Elli now, smiling easily. "And Elli. It's good to see you, but surprising under these circumstances."

"Thank you," she replied carefully.

"Mr. Black, I'm going to talk to you about your sister's condition, but as you can understand there was significant concern about her baby."

"Yes, she left Darcy with me yesterday," Wyatt offered. Elli noticed he didn't elaborate on how Barbara had left her. He was trying to protect his sister. Every time there was a development, Elli could see how Wyatt took on the responsibility himself. It was admirable, but she imagined it must be a very heavy load to carry at times.

"At what time?"

"Late morning," he replied without missing a beat. He met the doctor's eyes steadily. "I'm not used to babies, so Elli has been giving me a hand." He smiled at Elli now, but the smile had an edge to it. He was nervous, she realized, and seeking her support.

She smiled back at him, and then at Dr. McKinnon. "Between the two of us, we've muddled through."

"Darcy does need to be examined, though." Dr. McKinnon was firm. "Elli, I'm going to have Carrie show you to a curtain and we'll have the peds on call come down. In the meantime, I can speak to Mr. Black about his sister."

McKinnon's voice softened as she rose and stopped to touch the downy crown of Darcy's head. "Would that suit, young lady?"

Darcy's answer was to pop two fingers into her mouth and start sucking.

"I'm afraid she's hungry," Elli replied. "Could someone heat a bottle for me?" She no longer had access to the rest of the department, nor did she want it. Her presence had already been noted, she suspected. People here knew her. There would be questions and murmurings when she showed up with a baby in tow. She knew how it looked. Granted, it was awkward considering Tim was still on staff. But her job loss had been cutbacks, pure and simple.

She wondered if she'd stayed married to Tim if it would have made a difference when it came to the chopping block. Then she wondered if she would have wanted it to. She had just enough pride to know the answer right away. Despite the financial hardship, being made redundant was a blessing, freeing her to begin again.

She resolutely clipped Darcy back into her seat and picked up the bag of supplies. Well, let them talk. It wouldn't change anything. She didn't work here anymore, wouldn't have to see these people on a regular basis like before. She was starting over.

"I'm sure that can be arranged. I'll be right back, Mr. Black."

She opened the door and Wyatt stood. "Stay with her," he said to Elli. There was a fierceness in his voice. "I'll come find you."

Her heart thumped at his words, knowing he meant them. Even knowing he meant them for Darcy, the effect was the same. It made her feel warm, protected. Wyatt would do whatever was in his power to protect them both.

She'd never met a man quite like him before.

"I won't leave her side," Elli promised, wishing she could touch him somehow to reassure him. She was too shy to do such a thing beneath the gaze of an old colleague, so she offered a small smile instead and cast her gaze down, following Dr. McKinnon out the door.

At the desk her friend Carrie hung up the phone. "Ellison." She got up and came around the desk, giving her a quick hug. "Gosh, it's good to see you."

"Hello, Carrie." Elli couldn't help but smile at the warm reception. Of all the staff, Carrie had been the one who'd remained the most normal when it came to Elli's ordeal. "Interesting circumstances, huh?"

The clerk's face broke into a wide grin in response. "You know the E.R. Something needs to break up the boredom."

"Can you show Elli to a curtain, Carrie? And page Dr. Singh—we need to do a physical on the baby." Dr. McKinnon smiled at Elli. "It is good to see you again, Ellison."

She went back to continue her meeting with Wyatt while Elli and Carrie looked at each other.

"Let's find you a spot," Carrie suggested, and led the way through the twists and turns of the unit. She entered a curtained cubicle and put the car seat next to the bed.

"Thank you, Carrie. Could I trouble you to heat a bottle?"

"Of course you can. What a shock, though, seeing you here with a baby, when…"

But Carrie's voice drifted off and her cheeks colored. "I'm sorry, Elli. That was insensitive."

"You were going to say 'when it's so soon after William died.'"

"We were all so sad for you and Tim."

Funny, Elli realized—saying William's name had come more easily than she'd expected. And the mention of Tim didn't upset her as it might have. Maybe she had Wyatt to thank for that, too. If he hadn't asked for her help, she'd still be hiding away instead of facing things.

"It gets better," she said, trying a smile for Carrie's benefit. "I'm not sure I'll ever get over losing William completely, but at some point you have to start living again."

Elli stood rooted to the floor, dumbstruck. Had she actually said that? *Start living again?*

"Can't say as I blame you...your Mr. Black is pretty easy on the eyes."

Elli felt her body grow warm all over at the mention of Wyatt. "It's not like that...."

"What a shame."

She looked over and found Carrie watching her with an amused expression. "It's that obvious?"

"He's very good-looking. Tim would be jealous."

Elli shook her head. "I doubt it. It doesn't matter anymore anyway."

She realized she meant it. It didn't matter. How had all this happened since yesterday? Yesterday she'd merely been thinking about what to do next. Afraid of taking a wrong step.

"I'll go heat your bottle." Carrie tapped her arm lightly and scooted out of the cubicle.

Elli sat on the edge of the bed, covering her mouth in surprise. She thought of Wyatt's wild eyes as she'd opened her door and chuckled. "Well, I guess when you're thrown in the deep end, you have to swim," she murmured.

A few minutes later Carrie returned with the warmed bottle. "I wish I could stay and chat," she said, taking a quick moment to sit in the seat next to Elli. Elli picked Darcy up and cradled her in her elbow, then reached for the bottle. As Darcy began to suckle on the nipple, Carrie let out a sigh. "I've missed you. But I can only spare a minute. Forgive me, Elli, but...does it hurt? Just knowing?"

Elli didn't need help interpreting. Of course it hurt, knowing what she'd missed. She smiled wistfully at the young woman who had been her coworker for nearly two years. "A little. She's precious, isn't she?"

"A doll. And this Black, he's her uncle?"

Elli ignored the leap in her pulse at the thought of Wyatt. "Yes, and he lives next door to where I'm staying at the moment. Thank you for calling me today," she added. "We'd gone to Barbara's home to find her but came up with nothing."

"It was just a chance I took, after you called me last night. I'm glad it worked, though. That woman came in here all alone, poor soul. She needs someone in her corner."

And that someone was Wyatt. Elli could think of few better.

Darcy took in too much milk, coughed, spluttered and sent up a wail. At the same moment Carrie's pager went off.

"I've got to go."

"I'll be fine," Elli replied, settling down in the chair and giving Darcy the bottle once more.

Familiar sounds, hospital sounds, filtered through the curtains—the hushed footsteps of nurses and the quiet, confident tones of doctors. The odd moan or catch of breath of those in pain, and the sound of gurney wheels swishing on the polished floors. For a moment the memory of it was a bittersweet stab in her heart, a reminder of a past life that she'd once considered perfect. She was at home here, the sounds and smells so familiar they seemed a part of her. Once she'd waited out a particularly tense bout of Braxton Hicks contractions and Tim had checked on her every ten minutes.

With a free finger Elli stroked Darcy's hair. She had to stop thinking about what might have been. It never *would* be. She was so tired of feeling sorry for herself. It was exhausting. Nothing she could do could bring her own precious baby back. Being with Wyatt and Darcy had made her face it head-on, making her want to get on with simply missing him rather than the futility of wishing for what she could never have.

She looked down into Darcy's face—the closed eyes with the lids that were nearly transparent, the way one tiny hand rested on the side of the bottle as if to keep it from disappearing. "Who knew," she whispered, "how important you'd turn out to be?"

The curtain parted and Wyatt stepped through, with Dr. McKinnon behind him. "How's she doing?"

Wyatt's eyes were troubled, but the fear had subsided slightly. She smiled up at him. "We're right as rain. How about you? What's the news on Barb?"

"I'm going to see her," he replied. He reached out to tuck the blanket more securely around Darcy's feet and Elli noticed his hand was trembling.

"Wyatt?"

He finished fussing with the blanket and looked up. "They're letting me visit her, and then…" He cleared his throat. "And then I have to talk to a social worker."

The tone of his voice made it sound like the seven tortures of hell. Wyatt was a private man—Elli had sensed it from the beginning. He'd been reluctant to give her any sort of details at all, skirting around issues to give her just enough answers. Elli knew that speaking to social workers was going to be intrusive at best.

She tried to smile reassuringly. "All signs point to her trying to get help, Wyatt. This is a good thing. And it fits with the letter she left you, don't you think?"

"I hope so. I just…I don't want her going into foster care, Elli."

"I know that, and they will, too. Once Darcy's had her checkup, I'll meet you. How about—the cafeteria downstairs?"

"Okay."

Elli was aware of Dr. McKinnon waiting for Wyatt and wished for some privacy so they could talk without being overheard. "Unless you'd rather I went with you." Elli doubted Wyatt was prepared for what he'd see in the psychiatric ward. "It's good she's admitted, but it's not an easy place to visit, especially the first time."

"Knowing you're caring for Darcy is all I need," he responded, his gaze sliding away from her. "I'll find you once I've spoken to her."

He looked so uncomfortable her heart went out to him. She stood, Darcy resting along her shoulder, and went to stand in front of him. He was desperately trying to do the right thing, and he hadn't seen his half sister in years. These were hardly optimum circumstances for a reunion.

Damn the doctor and whatever scuttlebutt was filtering through the unit. Elli didn't care anymore. She lifted her free hand and touched his cheek lightly. "It will be fine," she murmured. "Darcy's safe and Barbara is in good hands."

He placed his hand over hers, sandwiching it between his palm and his cheek. It was warm there and soft, with only a slight prickle of stubble from his jaw. "Why are you being so helpful, Ellison? This is not your problem." He closed his eyes for a few moments as he inhaled and exhaled slowly.

"Because I can see you're trying to do the right thing and at great personal sacrifice."

Without saying another word, he turned her palm, pressed a quick kiss into it. His lips were warm and firm in contrast to the stubble on his chin. Emotions rushed through her at the tender gesture, so sweet and so unexpected.

He cleared his throat and squared his shoulders. "The cafeteria," he reminded her, and without another word left the curtained area.

Elli pressed her hand to her lips, shocked at the intimate touch, flustered, and...my word. She was pleased.

This wouldn't do. Wyatt was only reacting to the situation. He had said it himself. He was thanking her for helping, that was all. Everyone's emotions were running high. She couldn't read too much into it.

She struggled to remember that he'd never had any interest in getting to know her before Darcy had come on the scene. They'd been neighbors for two months and had crossed paths only once. And yes, maybe they were getting to know each other better, but she also knew that if they'd met elsewhere—on the street, in a shop—his head wouldn't have been turned. Heck, he'd shouted at her the first day they'd met. She was still carrying around an extra ten pounds she'd put on during her pregnancy, and her looks were what she'd consider strictly average. The caress meant little when she put it in perspective.

She took a moment to change Darcy's diaper, slightly more comfortable with the task than yesterday as she dealt with sticky tabs and squirming, pudgy legs. In less time than she might have imagined, Darcy was dressed and happy. Elli took out a rattle and smiled as the baby shook it in her tiny fist.

The curtain parted once more and Dr. Singh entered. He saw Elli and his face relaxed into a pleased expression. Then his gaze dropped to Darcy, kicking and cooing on the white sheets of the bed.

There was a flash of consternation on his face and Elli felt a sickening thud in the pit of her stomach. She'd conveniently forgotten why she'd avoided coming to the hospital over the past few months. Now she remembered. She hadn't wanted to have to deal with explanations and platitudes. Carrie was one thing; they'd been close friends. But every other person she knew in this hospital saw her as Elli who had married a doctor, carried his child, lost it, lost her marriage and finally her job. *Poor Elli.*

"I understand this is our missing Baby Paulsen." He covered the momentary awkwardness with a smile.

"Yes. Her name is Darcy."

"You brought her in?" He went to the bed and watched Darcy for a moment while Elli looked on anxiously.

"Yes and no. Darcy has been with Barbara Paulsen's brother, and he's a friend of mine. I've been giving him a hand."

"He must be a very good friend."

"A friend in need is a friend indeed," she quoted, trying to make light of it. She knew how it would look if she admitted they'd only truly become "friends" yesterday. But looking at the outside of a situation was rarely like looking at it from the inside, so she kept her mouth shut.

Elli waited while Dr. Singh gave Darcy a thorough check. He turned to her and smiled. "She's perfectly healthy," the doctor stated.

Elli stared into Dr. Singh's chocolate eyes, surprised at the concern she saw there. Was there something wrong with Darcy he hadn't wanted to say?

Dr. Singh sat on the edge of the bed and rested his hands on his white coat. "This isn't about Darcy," he said quietly. "It's about you, Elli. I want to know how you're doing since William's death."

His quiet concern ripped at her insides at the same time as it was comforting. People didn't know what to say to her—she got that. But no one asked how she was, or spoke

William's name. Even today—it was the first time she'd been able to say his name without her voice catching. To everyone else he was always called "the baby," as if he'd never been named. As if keeping him nameless would make it somehow easier. It wasn't.

"I'm doing okay. Better now." She was happy to realize it was true.

"How did you end up caring for Darcy?"

"Wyatt didn't know what to do," she said, trying to lighten things by giving a light laugh. "Of course, neither did I, really, but I was conveniently just next door." She smiled then, genuinely. "Tell me, Dr. Singh, how can a person resist an adorable face like that?" She motioned toward Darcy, who seemed intent on the rattle clenched in her tiny fist. The pieces clacked together as she shook her pudgy hand. Only, Elli knew it wasn't just Darcy's adorable face that counted. Wyatt's was becoming more of a pleasure each time they were together.

Dr. Singh smiled. "You can't. I just want to make sure you're okay with this. I know you must be grieving still."

Elli swallowed, but was surprised that the tears she expected were nowhere to be found. When was the last time before today that she'd thought of William without crying? She was getting stronger. "I am grieving, of course. But it's different now, and I think helping care for Darcy is good for me. I can't always wish for what will never be. I have to look forward rather than backward."

"Good." Dr. Singh put his hands on his knees and boosted himself up. "I am glad to hear it. It is good to see some roses in your cheeks, Ellison."

The roses bloomed pinker than before, because Elli knew it was Wyatt and his caress that had put them there. And she didn't want to start having feelings for him. She was finally just starting to get a handle on her emotions.

The last thing she needed was to get mixed up with some-one again. To rebound.

Maybe she should just look upon this time as a lovely gift. For the first time in months she felt alive.

"Thank you, Dr. Singh. Wyatt will be involved with social services because I know he wants to look after Darcy until Barbara can again. Would it be okay if he listed you as her pediatrician?"

"By all means."

Elli gathered her things. "It was good to see you, Doctor."

"And you." He smiled, then left the room with a flap of his white coat.

Now at loose ends, Elli realized she hadn't eaten all day. When there was no sign of Wyatt in the cafeteria, she hefted the car seat and made her way to the coffee chain near the west doors. A steamed milk and a muffin would do the trick, she thought. Carrying the paper bag and car seat while balancing a hot drink took more dexterity than she'd expected, and she went slowly back to the cafeteria, where she could at least sit down and wait.

When she returned to the entrance of the cafeteria, she came face-to-face with Wyatt. It took only two strides of his long legs before he caught up to her. "Where have you been?" He whispered it, but there was a hard edge to the words, so very different than the last time he'd spoken to her.

"I just went to buy a steamed milk," she explained, feeling the color drain from her face at his thunderous expression.

"Your timing stinks." He ground out the words.

"Is there a problem?" A woman's voice came from beyond Wyatt's shoulder and Elli closed her eyes. She'd disappeared with Darcy at the same time Wyatt had come to find her with...

"Ellison Marchuk, this is Gloria Hawkins from Child and Family Services."

Elli handed Wyatt the hot cup, her appetite lost. "Ms. Hawkins," she said quietly, adjusting Darcy's weight and holding out a hand.

CHAPTER SIX

I<small>T WAS PAST DARK BY</small> the time they arrived home again, and on the drive Wyatt had taken the time to cool down. Now he stared around his house with new eyes. In the space of little more than a day his whole life had changed. This run-down bungalow and farm had been enough for him. He'd bought it seeing the potential, and he had lots of time to fix it up the way he wanted. Or so he'd thought.

But this was a bachelor's house, sparsely decorated and functional. He had to make it a home, somewhere welcoming and comfortable rather than a simple place to lay his head. There was more at stake. It needed to be a place for *family*. No matter what happened, he had family now.

Elli was in the kitchen, cooking some sort of chicken dish for dinner. Already he could see small changes in the house, and it put him off balance. His desk was tidy—pens in a can she'd unearthed from somewhere. She'd gone through and straightened what things he had, giving the house a sense of order that seemed foreign. He shouldn't feel as if Elli was taking over—he knew that. She was going above and beyond with helping. But somehow he did. As though the house wasn't his anymore.

Darcy was watching from her spot in the car seat, her dark eyes following Elli's every move from stovetop to counter. Wyatt stood at the doorway, nursing a beer, fighting the false sense of domesticity. It was all temporary, not real. Darcy was not his child, and Elli was not his wife. It was a short-term situation. Before long things would go back to normal.

He couldn't deny he'd had flashes of attraction over the past day and a half, but he wasn't truly interested in Elli. Elli didn't care for him either, he knew. Anything that had happened so far was because of the extraordinary position they were in. When everything settled, they'd each go back to their own lives. He got the feeling that she was too much of a city girl to want the isolated life in the country for long. He couldn't get used to seeing her here. Darcy, on the other hand, was his niece. As things played out, he knew he wanted to have a home where she and Barbara could come to visit as often as they liked.

His mom would have wanted that. She would have wanted him to accept Barbara and make her welcome. Despite her difficult life, he didn't know anyone with as generous a heart as his mother.

But for now, this was reality, until Barbara was well enough to look after her daughter. There was work to do to make this a family home. He'd promised it to the caseworker at the hospital. He'd been so nervous, afraid she would take Darcy away into foster care anyway. And he'd growled at Elli for not being there right away. She had done nothing wrong. Instead Elli had been calm, and she had been the one who had carried the meeting. She'd been composed and articulate and reassuring when Wyatt had been scared to death. He wouldn't let that happen again.

"Do you like squash?"

Elli's voice interrupted his thoughts and he straightened. "Yeah, I guess."

"You guess?" She finished wiping a spoon and put it down on the counter. Her blue eyes questioned him innocently, but he knew there was little of innocence in his thoughts. Lord, but she was beautiful. Not in a flashy way either. At first her looks seemed ordinary. But they grew on a man—the glowing complexion, the blond streaks in her hair. The way her clothes seemed to hug her curves and how those curves caught his eye. Most of all, it was her eyes. Elli wasn't his woman, but those eyes got him every time.

He'd looked into them earlier today and had forgotten himself. That caress in the E.R. had been a mistake, brought on by her understanding and the fact that she was simply there for him. He'd felt it again when he'd tried to explain to the caseworker why keeping Darcy was so important to him, while still protecting himself. He'd fumbled the words, but Elli had put her hand on his arm and smiled at him.

"My mom used to bake squash in the oven," he said, coming forward and putting his empty beer bottle beside the sink.

Elli smiled, her face a sea of peace and contentment. She looked so at home, so…happy. He wondered how it could be so when he'd dragged her into this situation, turning her life upside down as well as his.

"I can do that," she answered. "As soon as I find a baking dish."

He found her a proper pan and put it on the counter. "You like to cook," he stated, starting to relax. His version of cooking consisted of baked potatoes and frying a steak.

"I do," she answered, still smiling. She took a small squash and quartered it, scooped out the middle and slathered the orange surface with a paste of brown sugar and butter. She slid it into the oven beside the chicken in mere seconds. "My mom taught me how to cook when I was just a girl. It was one of the things we did together. I make a wicked cabbage roll. Though I've never quite mastered the technique of her perogies. She makes them from scratch and they're the best thing I've ever eaten."

Wyatt leaned back against the counter and nudged Darcy's hand with his finger. The baby grabbed it and batted her hand up and down while Wyatt smiled. He liked her—when she wasn't crying. A baby's needs were uncomplicated and he liked that. Food, a dry bottom and love, he supposed. A simple love, a warm place to cuddle into and feel safe.

At that moment he missed his mother with an intensity that shocked him. It had been five years, but now and again the grief seemed to come from nowhere. His finger stopped moving with Darcy's and he swallowed.

"Wyatt?"

Elli was watching him curiously. "Are you okay? You look funny all of a sudden."

He shook off the sadness. What had come over him? He never indulged in sentimentality. Maybe it was Elli. She reminded him of his mother, he supposed. His mom had been the one to make their house a home when he was growing up, and he realized Elli was doing the same thing now with him, and Darcy.

"I was just remembering my mom," he replied carefully. "You remind me of her, you know. She was always cooking and smiling. I didn't realize how much I missed it."

Her smile faded and a tiny wrinkle formed between her brows. "I remind you of your *mother?*"

Apparently that wasn't what she had expected to hear. Belatedly he realized that most women wouldn't find that an attractive comparison. He stumbled over trying to find the right words to explain. "Only in the very best ways, Elli. She was the one who made our house a home. You're

doing the same thing for Darcy and me without even realizing it."

Damn it, was that pain on her face? What had he said
that was wrong? He was trying to pay her a compliment and
it was coming out all wrong. "I'm sorry if I said something
to upset you."

"You didn't," she murmured, but she wouldn't look him
in the eye anymore.

"Do you want to talk about it?"

He couldn't believe he was asking. But he'd heard
snatches of whispered conversations today. There was
more to Elli, and he found himself curious. The people
at the hospital where she'd worked knew. But she'd said
nothing to him about why her marriage had failed. And the
bits he'd heard left him with more questions than concrete
information.

"There's nothing to talk about," she insisted, moving
back to stir something on the stove. But he knew. She was
covering. He'd done it a thousand times himself.

"How did Barbara seem to you? You never said." She
still had her back turned to him, but there was a slight
wobble on the word *said*. He *had* touched a nerve. A part
of him wanted to pursue it and another part told him to
leave it alone. If she'd wanted to talk, she wouldn't have
changed the subject.

But he wasn't sure how to proceed. Talking about
Barbara was a loaded topic, too. The moment he'd entered
the hospital room Barbara had started crying and apologizing. Her doctor had gone with him, and Wyatt had let her
take the lead. Calm but compassionate. Problem was, Wyatt
had never seen himself as a very compassionate man.

So Barbara had cried and he'd held her awkwardly. She'd
apologized and he'd tried to say what he thought were the
right words—that the most important thing right now was

for her to get well. He'd insisted that Darcy was well taken care of.

"Seeing her was odd. She was like the Barbara I remembered, and yet she wasn't. There was an energy about her that wasn't quite right."

Elli nodded. "Her perspective is so skewed right now, and she's afraid. When I worked in the E.R.—"

She halted, but Wyatt wanted to know. She'd worked at the very desk where he'd checked in today. How had today affected Elli? It had been so hectic he hadn't asked.

"When you worked in the E.R.," he prodded.

"I was just going to say we saw lots of mentally ill patients. People who for one reason or another couldn't cope. That Barbara could recognize that in herself, that she checked herself in…" Elli met his gaze. "It was a brave thing to do. Certainly nothing to judge her for."

"Did I judge her?" He straightened in surprise. He hadn't, had he? Had he judged or simply been concerned?

"No, but I did. The moment I saw her note and saw Darcy. I'm sorry about that."

She turned back to the stove. Wyatt stared at her back for a few moments before stepping forward and simply putting a hand on her shoulder.

"So did I. I asked myself how a mother could do that to a child. Today I realized how much courage it took for her to do what she did."

"Thank you," Elli whispered.

He took his hand away, already missing the feeling of warmth that had radiated through his palm. He put his hand in his pocket instead. "Three times she asked where Darcy was. Eventually she got so agitated the doctor suggested I come back later. She reassured her that Darcy was getting the best of care. I felt a lot of pressure when he said that."

"You're doing the best you can, and she's got a clean bill of health. Don't be so hard on yourself."

But it was impossible not to be. It highlighted his failure as a brother, if nothing else. Maybe if he'd made an effort years ago, this would never have happened.

"She's going to be okay—that's the main thing. It was easier speaking to her doctor. She seemed very pleased that Barbara was asking about Darcy so much. That she'd taken steps to make sure the baby was looked after."

A memory flashed into his brain, of his mother when he'd graduated from high school. He'd been in a suit she'd bought on discount in Red Deer, and his father was nowhere to be found. *Don't think about your dad,* she'd said, taking his hand. *You remember this. Family is important. Don't let your dad teach you otherwise. Family is everything.*

She'd gotten tears in her eyes then. *You're everything, Wyatt.*

He realized now that she had to have known about Barbara all along. And still she'd stayed with his father. Why? He'd never know now.

"Asking for help is a positive sign," Elli agreed. She fiddled with a set of old pot holders.

"I should have been there," he replied, the confession taking a load off his shoulders. "I knew deep down she was my sister. I knew what had happened to her mother and I pretended she didn't exist. If only…"

"Don't." Elli's voice intruded, definitive and strong. "Do not blame yourself. You were a teenage boy. There is no before. There is only now." She blinked rapidly. "There is only now."

The words seemed to catch her up so completely his thoughts fled. "Are we still talking about Barbara? Or about you?"

His heart pounded as she turned her eyes up at him

once more. He couldn't resist her when she did that. Years of choosing to be alone hadn't made him immune to a beautiful woman. He could rationalize all he wanted, but the truth was he didn't want just any woman—he wanted her. He wanted a connection with another human being, something to anchor him so he didn't feel this was spinning out of control. Elli seemed to get to him without even trying.

He stepped forward, cupped her face in his hands and kissed her. All the self-recriminations vaporized; all the doubts fled in a puff of smoke. Nothing mattered for a few blissful seconds. There was only Elli, her soft skin, the moist taste of her lips, her body close to his. God, he'd needed this, badly. And when she made a soft sound in her throat, he deepened the kiss.

Surprise was Elli's first feeling, quickly chased away by the sensation of his lips on hers and his hands cradling her face like a chalice. Her emotions had been riding close to the surface all day, facing all the things she should have faced long before now. But she'd held herself together, through the hours at the hospital and even facing William's things at her mother's. Tonight, alone with him, the words had sat on her tongue burning to be said. And still she couldn't. But somehow he seemed to know anyway.

Oh, he smelled good. She could still smell the remnants of the aftershave he'd put on this morning, something simple and rugged. His lips were soft, the faint stubble on his chin was rough and the combination was electrifying. She heard a sound—coming from her own throat—and he deepened the contact in response.

She met him equally, nerves and excitement rushing in waves throughout her body as she slid her arms around his waist and put her hands on his back, pulling him closer.

The points where their bodies touched were alive and

she rejoiced, knowing it had been several long, lonely months since she'd felt such an intense connection with anyone. Elemental, raw and feminine.

He gentled the kiss, sliding his hands over her shoulders and down her arms as his lips parted from hers. His mouth hovered mere inches away from hers as their breath came rapidly, the sound echoing in the quiet kitchen.

"Why did you do that?" She whispered it, but the syllables sounded clearly in the silence. His kiss had made her feel like a woman again. But she wanted to hear him say it. She needed him to admit to the chemistry. She had despaired of ever feeling it again, of inspiring it again in a man.

"I don't know what came over me."

For once, Elli refused to let her inner voice speak. She knew what it would say—that he didn't find her attractive. The inner voice would make excuses. But she didn't want excuses. She wanted to believe in the power of the action itself. She wanted to believe in the attraction she'd felt humming between them.

She desperately needed to believe she'd been worth it. As long as he didn't apologize. She couldn't bear that.

"So it was because…" His hands rested on her arms and she kept hers about his waist. She wanted to keep touching him, just a few moments longer. He was so warm and strong.

"You keep looking at me and I—"

He broke off, pushed backward and dropped his hands.

"You?" she prompted. She wanted him to say the words. Her whole body begged him.

"I couldn't seem to help it."

The sweetness of it filled her. This was what she'd been missing. How long had it been since she'd felt desirable?

How long had she been picking apart things she'd done, words she'd spoken, how she looked? Her hair was too flat, her bottom too wide. She still carried weight around her middle from her pregnancy. But handsome Wyatt Black didn't seem to care about any of it.

His gaze probed hers. "But it was probably a mistake. We can't let this complicate things, Elli. We have to put Darcy first."

And just like that the bubble popped, taking the fizz out of the moment. Of course they needed to put Darcy first. He'd told the caseworker that she was a friend helping him care for his niece. He'd stressed how Darcy was the focus for both of them at this moment, and how having two people was vastly better than one. The baby was first priority. And that was as it should be. She was letting her vanity get in the way.

But it hurt. And she didn't know why. It shouldn't matter. Where would it lead? Nowhere. He was absolutely right.

"Of course we do." She gathered her wits and retrieved the pot holders, then went to the oven and took out the chicken. It *did* matter and she *did* know why. She was seeing a new side to Wyatt and she liked it. She was starting to care about him.

"Elli—I don't know how to thank you for all of this." He looked down at Darcy and Elli's heart wrenched at the tenderness in his face. Did he realize he was half in love with his niece already?

She should be thanking *him*. For pulling her out of her half existence and giving her a purpose again. For feeling, for the first time in months, like a woman. But she couldn't say any of that without explaining what came before, so she merely replied, "You're welcome."

Silence was awkward so she made herself busy, filling a

plate for each of them, and with Darcy napping, they took them to the table.

The light was low and so were their voices as they discussed what had happened at the hospital. It wasn't until Wyatt suggested she stay over that she had a moment of pause. A big moment.

"What do you mean, stay over?"

Wyatt put down his fork. "We told the caseworker that you were helping me, right?"

"Well, I know, but…"

"But I have livestock to look after as well, Elli. I know she is my responsibility, but I can't see how I can be up with her all night and work all day." He paused, looked down at his plate and back up again. "We should discuss your wage. I don't expect you to do this for nothing. You've done more than enough the last two days."

Elli's face flamed. That wasn't where she wanted this to go, a discussion of money. "We can talk about it later."

"But Elli…"

"There's no rush, Wyatt. Helping you with Darcy is not taking me away from anything more important, I promise."

"Then you'll stay?"

The idea was so seductive. She wouldn't admit it, but the Camerons' house was big, beautiful and incredibly lonely. Here at Wyatt's, despite the general frayed-around-the-edges look, there was life and conversation and purpose. But what would she be getting into? She had just admitted to herself that she was starting to care for Wyatt. *He'd kissed her.* Being here 24/7 was just setting herself up for hurt down the road.

"I'm right next door if you need me."

His gaze pinned her for several seconds before he picked up his knife and fork and started eating again. He'd taken exactly two bites before he put them down again, the clink of silverware against plate loud in the uncomfortable silence.

"Is this about me kissing you just now, Elli?"

She didn't want to look up, but she couldn't help it. His eyes were completely earnest—not angry, but probing, as if he was trying to understand. But of course, he couldn't.

"No, Wyatt, honestly it's not." It was only a partial lie.

"You can have the bed," he said, his voice low and rough. "I don't mind sleeping on the couch."

"Wyatt…" He was making it so difficult. How could she sleep in the bed, knowing he was just down the hall, folded up on the short sofa? The very thought of it made her heart beat a little faster. "I can help you, but you have to understand…I have assignments due. I'm taking some bookkeeping courses." It was a paltry excuse; she'd just got through telling him she had nothing pressing. She could easily do the assignments on her laptop and log in to the Camerons' wireless connection to send them in.

He was silent for several long moments. Elli looked up in surprise when he straightened his shoulders and squared his jaw. He looked like a man about to face his executioner, like one who was about to say something very unpleasant and the words were souring in his mouth. Butterflies swirled in her stomach.

"Elli, the one thing I cannot do is let that baby go into foster care. I promised. And I cannot do it alone. I barely got a few hours' sleep last night. I need you, Elli. I will not let that baby be taken away by child services. *I need you.*"

She tried to push away the rush of feeling that came upon hearing the words. She hadn't known him long, but she'd thought him too proud, too stubborn to admit such a thing.

He didn't need *her*—she understood that. He needed the help, but not her. She was, however, the one person who was here. And the assignments were an excuse. She'd been waiting for a chance to do something important, so what was holding her back? A crush? Didn't she trust herself enough to be smart?

Surely she could keep that in hand. Wasn't Darcy worth it? If it were William, wouldn't she want someone to do the same?

That was the clincher. Of course she would. She was in a unique position to help a child. To refuse for personal reasons was beyond selfish.

"What makes you think they would take her away?" Elli sipped on her water. Wyatt was more open now than he'd been. It could be a good opportunity to learn more about him. Why did the mere mention of a social worker tie him up in knots? Because even the way he said the words was as if they tasted bitter in his mouth.

"Look at this place." He pushed away his plate. "It is not the picture of a family home. I am not set up for a baby. I am a single man with no experience with infants. All that is working against me. I can't give them more ammunition. I need to make this place into a family home."

"You realize that they aim to keep children with families, right? That you're on the same side?"

But Wyatt shrugged it off. "Maybe so, but there are no guarantees. You don't know what it does to a kid to be taken away."

Her heart ached at the pain in his voice. "Darcy is only a few months old. She wouldn't remember, Wyatt."

"How do you know that? How do you know someone else will be kind? What happens with Barbara? Do you know what the doctor said? She said that Barbara had taken steps to make sure Darcy was safe. She removed herself from the situation. She put Darcy in the care of someone she trusted. Despite being ill she made decisions based on good mothering. I will not betray that faith she placed in me."

"Wyatt." Elli tried to contain her shock at his vehement words. She reached across the table and laid her hand over his wrist. His pulse hammered beneath her fingers as the bits clicked into place.

"When did it happen?" She asked it gently.

Wyatt turned his head to the left and looked out the window at the approaching darkness. "What are you talking about?"

She squeezed his wrist. "How old were you when you were taken away?"

He started to push back from the table, but she kept her hand firmly on his wrist. He paused halfway up, then sat back down. And this time when he met her gaze there was defiance, an I-dare-you edge in the dark eyes.

"I was nine."

"Oh, Wyatt."

"I was gone for a whole week. That's all. It was too long. I ran away twice trying to get back home. They let me go back when he promised."

"Promised what?" Elli felt slightly sick, afraid of what the answer was going to be, sad for the little boy he must have been.

"Promised he wouldn't hit me again."

Her mouth tasted like bile. "Did he?"

"No. Not with his fists, anyway. But he'd done enough. I always knew what he was capable of."

"Weren't you afraid to go home?"

He turned his hand over, studied her fingers, twined his with them. She wondered if he even realized he was doing it, twisting a connection between them as his jaw tightened.

"I couldn't leave my mother back there," he said simply. "I had to be with her. We only had each other, you see. Who does Barbara have if not me? Who does Darcy have?"

Elli's eyes smarted. Over in the baby seat Darcy started to snuffle and squirm, waking from her nap. Wyatt held hurts as deep as her own. So much made sense now, including his burning need to get it right. Did he think he was like his father?

"Wyatt, you could never be like him, you know that, right?"

His gaze was tortured as it plumbed the depths of her face. "How do I know that? When Darcy cries and I don't know how to make her stop…"

"You walk the floor with her. You came to me for help. Don't you see? You're doing a fine job with her. You're patient and loving. You're twice the man he ever was, Wyatt, I just know it."

His gaze brightened before he looked away.

"Okay. I'll move some things over. You won't have to worry about Darcy being taken away from you."

Relief softened the lines of his face. "Good. Because we still have to prove it at the social services home visit."

He rose and took his plate to the sink, then stopped at the seat and picked Darcy up, cradling her protectively against his chest.

How was Elli supposed to come through unscathed now?

CHAPTER SEVEN

WHEN ELLI RETURNED from the Camerons' house with a bag, Wyatt was in the middle of the living-room floor, setting up the playpen they'd brought from her mother's. His dark head was bent in concentration, his wide hands working with the frame. Elli caught her breath and held it, pushing past the flare of attraction. She almost welcomed the stab of grief that came in its wake as she glimpsed the brightly colored pattern on the nylon. Darcy. The playpen had been meant for William, and she couldn't quite squelch the anger and pain, knowing he would never use it.

But why shouldn't Darcy have it now? Wasn't it better that it was going to be put to some use?

Wyatt fiddled with a corner and mumbled under his breath. Elli left her maudlin thoughts behind and smiled at his grumbling. "Having fun?"

Wyatt looked up, a wrinkle between his brows and a curl of hair out of place, lying negligently on his forehead. There it was again—the buzz of excitement. She bit down on her lip.

"There are way too many buttons and levers on baby things," he replied. He stood, gave the side of the playpen a quick jerk and the frame snapped into place. "There. It might not be a crib, but at least for tonight she won't have to sleep in her car seat."

Elli put down her overnight bag and went to his side. A plush pad lined the bottom of the playpen, decorated in farm animals. Darcy lay on the floor next to him on an activity mat, her attention riveted on a black-and-white zebra with tissue paper crinkling beneath the fabric.

"You're trying really hard." Elli knelt beside him and rested her hand on the nylon of the pen. In the short time she'd been gone she could see he'd tried to tidy up the living room. A lamp glowed warmly in the back corner and he'd put a soft blanket over the sofa cushions, covering the worn upholstery. The room was more homey than she'd thought, and the warm light highlighted a framed Robert Bateman print on one wall. It was a fine house, it was just…neglected. It wouldn't take much effort to bring it up to scratch.

"I never really had a reason before," he said quietly, getting to his feet. "I've been on my own a long time." A ghost of a smile tipped his lips. "And in case you haven't noticed, I'm pretty low maintenance."

She laughed lightly, drawn in by the cozy light and the easy way he spoke, but beneath it all warning herself she couldn't get used to it. "And babies aren't."

"Certainly not." He went to another box, one they'd just managed to slide inside the trunk of her car. "I should put this together next." As he opened the top flap, he carried on. "I can't thank you enough for arranging the loan. This stuff is brand-new! Where did you get it?"

She'd neglected to tell him that the house where they'd stopped belonged to her parents, and she'd determined ahead of time that should he ask she would simply answer that they belonged to someone who had lost a baby. The fewer details the better. She'd been spared explanations earlier, as on the drive home Darcy had been fussing.

The last thing she wanted was to tell him what had really

happened with William. But after his own revelation at
dinner, she felt compelled to be honest with him. Maybe
if she gave him just a bit of the truth, it would be enough
to stop his questions. She had to talk about it sometime.
Maybe then it would get easier.

"It was for me, for when I had a baby," she said, determined to keep her voice even. She didn't want to see the
same pity on his face that she'd seen today at the hospital,
facing her old coworkers again. The last thing she wanted
from Wyatt was his pity. "I stored it at my mom's, that's all.
You know mothers. You mention the word grandchild…"

He slid a flat board out of the box and put it to the side.
"Wasn't that jumping the gun a little bit?" He said it easily,
even teasing, but Elli was finding it hard to keep up the pre-
tense. The logic of her decision to skim the surface made
perfect sense, but she wasn't quite as successful at stifling
the emotions that came into play. When she didn't answer,
Wyatt looked up. His smile faded and those damnably dark
eyes searched hers yet again.

"I've said something wrong."

He got up off the floor and went to her, not touching
her, but she could see the wall of his chest and she blinked.
She would not cry. Not again. She'd cried enough, and
she'd done so well today. At some point she had to talk
about it without falling apart. Wyatt didn't come with any
preconceived notions about her, or her marriage to Tim.
And once she left the Camerons' house, their paths would
likely never cross again.

"It's all right," she said quietly. "You couldn't have
known."

"What happened?"

"I was pregnant but…" She didn't want to go into too
much detail. Concern was one thing, and it was already
written all over his face. Full disclosure would bring the

pity and sympathy. She'd decided to tell him, so why was it so difficult to say the words? "But I lost the baby," she finished on a whisper, unwilling to elaborate further. "All the things we'd bought we put at my mother's, thinking they'd still be there later."

"But there was no later," he guessed.

She kept staring at the buttons of his shirt, noticing oddly that their color matched the fabric precisely. "No, there wasn't," she answered softly. "Our marriage ended."

And so did the dream, she thought, but the idea wasn't as sad as it might have been. Tim had married her for the wrong reasons. He'd wanted a good wife, a home in a prestigious neighborhood and the picture-perfect family to go with it. In that, they'd been alike. She'd fancied herself in love with him when she'd been in love with her own dreams instead. It wasn't a mistake she planned to make again. She was stronger now. If she ever married again, it would be for nothing less than the real thing.

"I'm sorry," he said, and while Darcy stared intently at a blue elephant on the play mat, Wyatt took Elli into his arms.

It felt so good to be held there, nearly as good as his kiss had felt earlier. His chest was warm and solid, his arms gentle around her. It had been so long since she'd allowed herself to lean on anyone at all that she sighed, feeling a weight lift from her shoulders.

"Don't be sorry. It's not your fault," she murmured, knowing she should pull away but not quite ready to give him up so soon. She hoped that would be the end to the questions. He could go on thinking she'd had a miscarriage and that would be it. He didn't need to know how close to her due date she'd been, so close she could taste the sweetness of motherhood, only to have it ripped cruelly away.

His wide palm stroked her hair and a shiver went down

her spine, a feeling of pure pleasure. A gurgle sounded from the mat as Darcy discovered a new texture.

"The last two days and you didn't say anything. I saw your expression a few times as you tended to Darcy and knew there was something, but…" He pushed her away from him so he could look into her face. Not pity there, then. No, it was pure compassion, and she felt her determination to keep him at arm's length slip another notch. "If I had known…how callous of me," he finished, squeezing her hands.

"I could have said no." She smiled a little, squeezing back. "You and Darcy needed help. You couldn't have known."

Darcy grew tired of being ignored, and squawked. Wyatt let go of Elli's hands and went to the baby, picked her up in his wide hands and rested her in the crook of his arm.

"Yesterday I was terrified to touch her, and already she seems to settle when I hold her."

"You're a natural." Elli smiled, glad to leave the topic behind. She reached up to adjust Darcy's shirt.

"Hardly. But I want to do right by her. And if this is too much for you, I understand. I wouldn't have asked if I'd known how it would hurt you." Darcy's chubby hand grabbed at his lower lip. He removed her fingers gently and kissed them.

Elli was sure he hadn't consciously done it, but there was a tenderness to Wyatt that was utterly unexpected. It was in the way he'd put his arms around her, the way he held Darcy in his arms and vowed to fiercely protect her. She hardly knew him, but in some ways she already understood him better than she'd ever understood Tim. Tim had spoken to her as a doctor would, using technical terms and medical explanations. Wyatt didn't. He simply offered a genuine "sorry" and a hug.

"No, it's good for me. I should have stopped hiding away ages ago. I've put off moving on, and caring for Darcy is helping with that. It hurts, but you're not the only one benefiting from this arrangement."

"As long as you're sure…"

"I'm positive."

The atmosphere in the room seemed to lighten. "Okay, then, can you take her while I put this thing together?" Wyatt smiled, pushing the serious topics to the side and moving back to the present problem, and Elli was grateful. They'd learned something new about each other today and they were still standing. Her initial impression of him, the one where she'd labeled him a complete grump, wasn't bearing out. They were—to her surprise—becoming friends.

"Sure. She's due for a bottle anyway." Elli took Darcy in her arms, realizing she was getting used to her weight there, and liking it. As Wyatt organized hardware and parts, she went to the kitchen and heated a bottle, then came back to the living room, settling in the corner of the sofa. Darcy's warm weight relaxed in the crook of her elbow as she took the bottle, the blue eyes staring up at Elli with what felt like trust.

She sat quietly while Wyatt put together the change table. The silence was pleasant. Wyatt might think his home wasn't good enough, but it held something that many homes with better furniture and fresher paint didn't. It held comfort. A gurgling sound from the milk being pulled through the nipple made Elli smile.

How could it be that she felt more at home here than she had at her own condo with Tim? The thought disturbed her. How could she have been so wrong? How could she have fooled herself so well? Why had she settled when she'd really wanted something so much simpler?

"What do you think?"

Wyatt's voice pulled her out of her musings and she realized that he was standing proudly next to the change table. The maple-colored wood gleamed in the lamplight and a quilted pad fit on the top. No more changing Darcy on a sofa cushion or bed or whatever happened to be near. She had a place to sleep and now a table where they could organize her diapers and supplies. Darcy was settling in. And so was Elli. She wasn't yet sure if it was a good thing or not.

It felt right, which scared the daylights out of her. It would be fine as long as she kept up her guard. Then she'd find a new job, and an apartment somewhere. An apartment that she knew now would be more like Wyatt's home. Set up for comfort, not for style.

Darcy had fallen asleep and Elli put her down on the sofa. "It looks great," she said, going over to the table and running her fingers over the polished wood. "Where should we put it?"

Wyatt shifted his weight, suddenly awkward. "I suppose wherever she sleeps. The second bedroom still needs to be cleaned, and probably painted. I tried to get the rooms I needed livable first."

"And it doesn't feel right putting her in here."

"Well…"

"I still feel funny taking your room, Wyatt. I can sleep on the couch."

"No, I wouldn't feel right. You take the bed. I'm up at six for chores and I'd wake you."

"Then I can keep Darcy in with me."

"You're sure?"

"Yes, I'm sure. Isn't that why you wanted my help? So you can look after your livestock and I can look after Darcy?"

"Yes, but I..."

"Feel guilty."

A small smile played on his lips. "Something like that."

"I can take care of myself, Wyatt."

"Will you let me know if you need anything, then?"

"Do you always try to take care of everyone?"

His gaze slid back to hers and she remembered the way he'd drawn her into his arms, the way his lips had felt against hers. She was determined to make her own way this time, but there was something alluring about the thought of being looked after by Wyatt Black.

"Is that a fault?"

She couldn't help but smile, her heart tripping along a little faster than normal. "That's the standard 'answer a question with a question' technique. But I'll let you off the hook this time. We've got more important things at hand. There's a small matter of needing baby things," she said, taking a step away. Being close to Wyatt was becoming a habit and one she had to break. "We're on our last outfit, and nearly out of diapers. The can of formula I bought isn't going to last, either. If you start a list, I can run into town in the morning and do some shopping."

"That would be very helpful, but I don't want you to feel—"

Elli interrupted, laughing. "Stop it. You asked me to help and what, now you feel guilty about it?"

"You're teasing me." He said it with surprise, and Elli felt a frisson of pleasure skitter along her spine. It did wonders for her confidence to know she could put him off his balance.

"Maybe a little. You're so serious, Wyatt. You need to relax."

Wyatt fiddled with the screwdriver, finally putting it

back in a leather pouch. "I don't mean to be so serious," he confessed.

Elli recognized it not only in him but herself lately, as well. Maybe they both needed to lighten up. These little exchanges with him definitely made her feel better.

"You're concerned about the home visit, right? So let me do this, get the basics covered while you worry about work. A girlie shopping trip is just what Darcy and I need." She rubbed her hands together.

A quiet pause filled the room. She exhaled and continued in a calm, logical tone. "Isn't that why you asked me to stay?"

"I know you're right," he conceded. "About the necessities, anyway. And if it means I don't have to shop…" He strode off to the kitchen and Elli followed, stopping when she heard the tinny sound of a coffee can. Wyatt had relaxed for a few minutes, but now his jaw was set again in what she was beginning to recognize was his stubborn look. He took a wad of bills out of the can and started counting it off.

"How much do you think you'll need?"

Elli gaped. "You keep your money in a *coffee can?*"

"This is my emergency fund. It's easier to give you the cash than it is to sort out banking cards or credit cards." He held out several bills. "Take it and get what you need tomorrow. I don't dare take another day away from the stock, and you're right. It will be a huge help."

She reached out and took the money. "Okay, then."

He put the lid back on the can and returned it to a low cupboard. Elli frowned. Wyatt resorted to a can? It seemed so…old-fashioned. Just when she thought she was starting to puzzle him out, something else cropped up that made him a mystery. Maybe she should just stop trying.

"Come on," he said, turning back to face her, the earlier

stubbornness erased from his features and replaced with a smile. "Let's get the two of you settled."

Elli was following him down the hallway and his heart was beating a mile a minute. He didn't know what to do about Elli anymore. She was such a puzzle. Wounded and emotional one moment, teasing him the next. He couldn't forget the expression on her face when she'd told him about the miscarriage. It all made sense now. The odd looks that shadowed her face at times, the way she had first handled Darcy, as if she was afraid. And then…oh, God. The comment he'd made yesterday about all girls wanting babies. What an ass he was. He wanted her help, wanted her to feel at home and her confession made him feel like a heel.

Inside the bedroom he suffered another bout of embarrassment. The room was, at best, plain. A bed and a dresser, nothing on the walls, nothing inviting or cozy as he'd expect a woman's room to be. He'd never put much thought into decorations or felt the need to clutter things up with objects that held no meaning. He supposed that philosophy made his place look a bit spartan.

"I'm sorry it's not very fancy," he apologized, seeing the room through her eyes.

"It's fine," Elli replied. "I expect you've put your energies into the ranch and not the decor."

As she put down her overnight bag, Wyatt stripped the white sheets off the bed and tossed them into a plastic hamper along the wall. "That about sums it up," he agreed. He wondered what she was thinking. He knew how the house appeared. The petty cash he kept in the kitchen probably didn't help. It wasn't as if he didn't have the money to fix things up. He'd just put his priorities elsewhere.

"I'll get some fresh sheets," he murmured, going to the hall closet. The couch wasn't going to be comfortable, but

Darcy was his niece, not Elli's. She had no reason to stay, but she was doing it anyway. She was his guest. And yet the thought of her sleeping in here, in his bed, Darcy in the playpen beside her, did funny things to his insides.

He hadn't expected an instant family, no matter how temporary. After years of solitude, it was odd to have others sharing his space. In particular Elli, with her shy smiles and soft eyes. She seemed to take everything at face value and didn't judge because of it. And in a few short days she seemed to be everywhere.

It almost made him want to explain things to her. Things he had never explained to anyone.

He returned with the sheets. Elli had put Darcy in the middle of the bed and he heard her coming behind him, carrying the playpen. She brought it into the room and smiled. "If I put it beside the bed, I can get to her easily when she wakes," Elli explained. "A flannel sheet underneath her and the blanket should be enough. The nights aren't too chilly yet."

She put the sheet on the mattress pad and Wyatt picked up Darcy, placing her gently on the soft surface. She blinked up at him.

Then he looked at Elli and felt his heart turn over. She was looking at the baby with such tenderness it hurt him. Now he knew she'd lost her baby and her marriage and her job. And yet she greeted life with a smile. It was more than he'd managed for many years. He'd spent a long time drifting around, working, making enough money to settle somewhere, never getting too close to anyone. He'd lost his entire family and he'd spent his time nursing his wounds. Perhaps he'd nursed them too much. Buying this place—making it into something profitable—was his way of moving on.

But now it was different. He had a family, even if it

wasn't quite the one he'd expected. And Elli was a part of it whether it made sense or not. He was surprised that he wanted her to be.

He smoothed the sheet over the mattress and pulled up the comforter. "Are you sure you'll be warm enough?" Elli's cheeks flushed a little and he was charmed. "There are extra blankets in the hall closet."

"This will be fine," she murmured. "You're going to need the blankets anyway."

"And a pillow. I hope you don't mind if I take one."

"Of course not." She stared at the bed again and the nerves in his stomach started jumping, just as they had in the kitchen before he'd kissed her. The temptation was there. He wondered what it would be like to lie beside her. In his bed. To feel her body close to his, to kiss her in the dark, to hear her whisper his name.

He grabbed the pillow. After everything that had happened today, his libido had to stay out of it. He wanted to ask her what had happened. He wanted to know how her husband could have let her get away, if he'd been there for her or not. By the way she'd melted in his arms, he'd guess not. Not the way she deserved.

"The bathroom is down the hall. I'll bring the change table in and then say good-night."

Elli nodded dumbly and the temptation to kiss her reared up again. But he put it off. She was still a little jumpy from earlier, and it felt wrong to press.

When he delivered the change table, Elli was sitting cross-legged on the bed, a book and a small laptop open in front of her. Darcy was there, too, on top of the covers with a ring of plastic keys clutched in her chubby fist. As Elli turned a page in the book, she absently rubbed Darcy's foot with her free hand.

Wyatt swallowed.

Why did having her here feel so right? Why had he felt like such a miser counting out bills to give her? He wasn't rich, but he had this place and he could certainly afford to put food on the table and buy the necessities. Maybe it was time he put some effort into the inside, bringing the house up to scratch.

Why couldn't he get her off his mind?

He put down the table along the far wall and looked at the two of them, so comfortable and so right. Odd that he'd spent so many years roaming around looking for the right opportunity and here it was, dropped into his lap. Darcy's arrival had thrown a kink into things, but he understood the reason now. It wasn't about the ranch or cattle or making his mark.

It was about family. And it was about Elli.

His mother, even when things were at their worst, had cautioned him not to be bitter. She had begged him not to judge the world based on his parents' marriage. He had anyway, for a long time.

But when he looked at Elli, those jaded thoughts seemed far away. She had obviously been through a lot and she was still smiling. Maybe he could make things better for her in a way he never could for his mom.

She put her hand on Darcy's tummy, rubbing absently, and the bubble burst. How could he be thinking about being with her when Darcy was his first priority? He had to ensure that Darcy stayed with him until she could be reunited with her mother.

"You're staying up for a while, then?"

Elli looked up from her book and smiled. "Darcy's not ready for sleep yet. If I finish this assignment, I can send it tomorrow."

He nodded. "Elli, about the money...you know where

the can is. What I'm saying is, take more if you think you'll need it."

"I don't want to spend you out of house and home," she replied, but she focused on her book instead of on him.

So that was it. Did she think he was so poor a few things were going to strap him? "That's just petty cash, Elli," he explained, putting his hands into his pockets and smiling. "You're not going to break the bank. Besides, I trust you."

That got her attention and she looked up. "You do?"

"Is there any reason I shouldn't?"

Her cheeks blossomed and he thought once more how pretty she looked.

"I did think about picking up a few things to spruce up the house a little, but wasn't sure how to ask."

"Of course. I'm hopeless when it comes to decorating. I think it's a guy thing. I'd be happy for you to pick up some stuff. It might help make things look nicer for when family services does their assessment."

He went to the door and rested his hand on the frame, not wanting to leave but feeling silly staying.

"Wyatt?"

"Hmm?" He turned back around, fighting the strange urge to kiss her good-night. Maybe it would be best if he just got the hell out of there.

"I won't take it all, don't worry."

"Do I look worried?"

She smiled an angelic smile and he clamped down on the desire that rushed through him. "Actually, yes."

"Not about that," he replied, and before he could change his mind, he closed the door behind him and went to make up the lumpy couch.

It didn't matter. He wasn't going to sleep tonight anyway.

CHAPTER EIGHT

ELLI DID A QUICK CHECK of the house to quell the nerves
dancing around in her stomach. The phone call had come
earlier than they'd expected. The social worker from
Didsbury was coming in the afternoon.

She was glad she'd gone shopping early that morning. A
cheery new tablecloth dressed up the kitchen and she had
also bought matching tea towels and pot holders. Wyatt
had finished the chores outside and just after lunch he'd
brought in his toolbox and fixed the sagging front door so
it opened and closed easily. Now he was taking a shower.
Darcy was bathed and sweet smelling and dressed in a new
pink two-piece outfit.

Elli now took a moment to brush her hair and twist it up,
anchoring it in the back with a clip. The refrigerator was
full and the house tidied. Darcy had enough formula for
several days, diapers stacked neatly on the change table,
and several cute, serviceable outfits. It had been a bittersweet pleasure shopping for them, picking them up and
choosing the patterns and styles. It was something she'd
never had the chance to do for William, and it had been
fun. She would have enjoyed the day out, regardless, as
she'd finally felt she had a purpose. She hadn't realized
how much she'd missed it until she was needed again.

But all in all she was nervous. Both for Wyatt, who

had a lot riding on this meeting, and for herself. She had been with Wyatt at the hospital and now at the house. She knew that she would also have to answer questions. And without knowing what the questions would be, she couldn't anticipate the answers. It wasn't even so much talking to a complete stranger. There seemed to be some safety in that. It was airing everything in front of Wyatt. She shouldn't care what he thought, but she did. His opinion mattered.

She heard the dull thump of Wyatt's stocking feet coming down the hall and she took one last glance in the mirror, forcing the worry lines from her face and pasting on what should look like a pleasant smile. She'd taken extra care with herself, too, dressing in navy slacks rather than her usual jeans, and a soft raspberry-red sweater. When she turned he was standing behind her, and the curve of her lips faltered the slightest bit at his appearance.

He was so handsome. Even in neat jeans and a blue-and-white-striped shirt, he still exuded that little bit of rough danger, of excitement. It was in his deep-set eyes and the just-a-bit-too-long tips of his dark hair. An air of carelessness, when she knew in many ways that *careless* was one of the last words she could use to describe him.

It made for an intriguing package.

"Do I look okay?"

Worry clouded his enigmatic eyes, and she reached out, putting a hand on his arm. "Of course you do."

"Maybe I should have dressed up more."

Elli tried to picture him "dressed up" and it wouldn't quite gel. He belonged in well-fitting jeans and cotton shirts that emphasized his broad shoulders. "I don't think so. This is who you are. And today of all days, you need to be yourself. You can't pretend to be someone you're not."

A furrow appeared between his brows. "Not helping," he replied, and Elli laughed.

"Who would you trust more? Someone who looked great but was clearly uncomfortable? Or someone who looked calm, capable and comfortable in their own skin?"

He moved his arm so that his fingers could twine with hers. A thrill skittered down the length of her arm at the simple touch.

"That's how I appear? Wow. I didn't realize these clothes had special powers." Finally a smile broke through his tense features. "You look nice, too. The red brings out the roses in your cheeks."

When Wyatt smiled Elli felt as if a candle had been lit inside her. Maybe because he didn't bestow his smiles frivolously and they seemed to mean more because of it. "You're teasing me," she accused softly, pleased he'd noticed her extra effort. She resisted the nervous habit of straightening her clothing. She'd had the sweater for ages and had never worn it, thinking it too bold. After last night, and with the social worker coming, she'd wanted Wyatt to see her in something other than her normal exciting-as-a-mushroom colors.

He nodded. "You look as nervous as I feel. You even put your hair up." His gaze roamed over the twist, held with a clip so that a few ends cascaded artfully over the top. "I like it. It makes you look…sophisticated." He let go of her fingers. "Too sophisticated for a run-down ranch in the boondocks."

But Elli had noticed things in the past weeks, too, even if it had just been from a distance, on the deck of the Camerons' house. "This place isn't run-down. You have already made a lot of improvements. It takes time and hard work."

Wyatt's keen gaze caught her once more. "Of anything I expected today," he said quietly, "I didn't expect that. I didn't expect your unqualified support. Thank you, Elli."

The sincerity in his voice made her want to hug him, but she could not. Would not. Sure, she could see the differences and yes, she was attracted to Wyatt. But once this "situation" was resolved he would be back to being a full-time rancher and she would be...not at the Camerons'. This was meant to be a time to forge her own new life, not be sucked into someone else's again as she had been with Tim.

Wyatt's kiss last night was just an indulgence in fantasy. It had been lovely, but she couldn't let it be a life-changing event. She did not want life-changing events. What she wanted was to rebuild and begin again, this time much stronger.

"You're welcome. And try not to worry so much. Darcy should be with you. You're her uncle. It's not like this is forever, either."

She said the words to remind herself as much as him. It would be far too easy to get caught up in the situation and mistake it for reality.

Both of them heard the car turn up the drive, and in concert they turned their heads toward the front door. "This is it," Wyatt murmured, and the wrinkle reappeared in the middle of his brow as Elli straightened her sweater. There was no time to recheck her makeup. She would have to do as she was.

Wyatt opened the door and stepped out onto the veranda. Elli noticed that while the paint was still peeling, there were several pieces of yellowy fresh lumber where Wyatt had shored up the steps and floor. Sometimes it seemed he could do anything with his hands and a few supplies.

A young woman barely older than Elli got out of the car. She was tall and dark haired, the straight tresses pulled back in an elegant sweep. There was nothing about the woman that was ostentatious or over the top, but she was the kind of put-together female who always made Elli feel just a bit dowdy. Now, with only a sheer layer of foundation and some lipstick for makeup, Elli felt the difference keenly. It made her want to fade into the woodwork.

Come to think of it—perhaps that wasn't such a bad idea. The less she was in the spotlight today the better.

She slipped back inside as Wyatt greeted the woman. "Miss Beck, I'm Wyatt Black. I'm glad you could come today."

Oh, he was smooth, Elli thought, envying how he could cover up all that nervousness with charm. She heard the higher sounds of the woman's reply and bit down on her lip.

The door opened and Wyatt held it for Miss Beck to come through. She stepped inside and looked around briefly before moving to unbutton her coat.

"I appreciate you being so accommodating," she said as Wyatt stepped forward to take the coat from her. He hung it on a peg behind the door and rubbed his hands together. Elli watched it all from the living room, where she quietly folded a load of towels she'd taken from the dryer only minutes before. Anything to keep her hands busy and not twisting together as she was tempted to do.

"There was no reason to put it off. Of course you want to make sure Darcy is well looked after. We want the same things, Miss Beck. The best of care for my niece while her mother recovers."

That earned a smile from Miss Beck. "So we do," she agreed. "Please call me Angela. I can't quite get used to Miss Beck. It makes me feel like a schoolteacher."

Wyatt smiled back and Elli held her breath. Perhaps this wasn't anything to be so nervous about. Perhaps the caseworker at the hospital had been unusually stern.

"Like any government agency, there is paperwork that

needs doing, and procedure we need to go over. Might I see Darcy first, though?" Angela suddenly noticed Elli in the living room. "Oh, hello."

Elli swallowed and felt even shorter than her five feet three inches and every ounce of her despised extra pounds. She tried standing taller and held out a hand. "Hello. I'm Ellison Marchuk."

"Elli is helping me out with Darcy," Wyatt explained. Angela nodded, but Elli didn't feel any easier. How would it appear? Like a friend? Like a girlfriend? Which did she prefer? She wasn't sure.

"Darcy's sleeping right now, but I could get her up. Or you could peek at her. I'm sure she'll be up soon."

"That would be fine."

Elli led the caseworker down the hall to the bedroom. She had made the bed and besides the playpen and change table she'd added a few velvety throw pillows to Wyatt's bed and a cute mobile of puppies and kittens in primary colors, attached to the side of the playpen. They both peeked over the side. Darcy was sleeping, covered to her armpits with the pink blanket and with both hands resting on either side of her head in a classic baby pose. Elli's heart twisted as she looked down at the peaceful face. Darcy had no idea of the turmoil going on around her. If Elli could do one thing, it would be to make this as easy on Darcy as possible so she never need suffer any long-lasting effects from being separated from her mother.

They tiptoed out and Angela turned to Elli. "She's a beautiful baby."

Elli nodded. "And good, too. Well, as good as you'd expect a newborn to be." She smiled. This woman felt like an ally. It would be all right. It had to be.

Wyatt was waiting in the kitchen, sitting at the table staring at his hands. When they entered he stood up.

"Shall we get started?" Angela Beck was all business now and she picked up her briefcase, taking out a file folder. "We need to work through your application first, Mr. Black."

The volume of papers she laid out was staggering. Wyatt looked at Elli and she felt his hesitation clear across the room.

"Is this all really necessary? It's such a short-term thing, after all."

"Perhaps, but perhaps not. We don't really know when your sister will be able to resume care for Darcy or how long you will be temporary guardian. Does that present a problem?"

Wyatt's hands unfurled and he looked her dead in the eye. "Absolutely not. Darcy can stay here as long as it takes. I'm the only family they've got and it's only right that Darcy stay with me until Barbara is well."

"Then let's proceed."

Elli went through the motions of putting on coffee while Wyatt and Angela worked through the application. She gave a cup to Angela, then fixed another the way Wyatt liked it and put it by his elbow. His shoulders were so stiff. Despite his easy smiles, she could tell he was wound up tighter than a spring. She put her hand on his shoulder for just a moment and squeezed.

The hands of the clock ticked on as Wyatt went through his orientation. Elli fed Darcy when she woke, changed her diaper and put a load of laundry in the washing machine. Finally Angela Beck tamped the papers together and put them into her briefcase. "That was great coffee. Why don't we take a minute and you can show me around, Mr. Black?"

Elli put Darcy in the new windup swing, and the motion ticked out a rhythm as she tidied up the few dishes in the sink. Wyatt gave Angela a brief tour, outlining how long he'd lived there and what improvements he'd already made to the property as well as what he had planned in the days ahead. "I'd focused more on the livestock and ranch when I first moved in," he explained. "But Darcy changes things."

"How so?"

They paused at the end of the hall and Elli held a cup in her hand, the dishcloth dripping water back into the sink, waiting for his answer.

"Having a child under your care changes your priorities, wouldn't you agree?"

"I would."

Elli carefully placed the cup in the drying rack. Did Wyatt know how rare he was? He wasn't putting on a show for the social worker as some people might. He was answering honestly, sincerely. No one could dispute his dedication to his niece, surprise appearance or not. He was a man who would do what needed to be done, a man who would do the right thing. He'd do anything for someone he loved, she realized. At personal sacrifice to himself. She didn't know many men like that.

"And Miss Marchuk, is it?" Angela Beck's astute gaze pinned her in place. Elli felt awkward and plain next to Beck's efficiency. Lord, the woman was well put together. Not a hair out of place, while Elli could feel a few flyaway pieces fraying around the edges of her face.

"That's right." She curbed the urge to say *Yes, ma'am.* Angela Beck couldn't be any older than Elli was.

"How long have you and Wyatt been living together, then?"

Elli felt her control slipping by the sheer surprise of the question. "Living together," she repeated, somewhat stupidly, then looked to Wyatt for guidance.

Angela raised an eyebrow. "Our eligibility requirements state that if there is cohabitation the relationship must be a stable one for the good of the child. We require a twelve-month minimum."

Wyatt couldn't be disqualified as a temporary guardian simply because she was here. It was wrong. "We're not living together," she replied.

"Oh?" The tone of Beck's voice said she didn't quite believe it.

"Ellison is the nanny," Wyatt supplied. He sent Elli a dark look and gave his head a slight shake just before Angela turned and looked at him.

"Your nanny?"

"Of course. I do have a ranch to run, and I needed help. Elli has agreed to help out temporarily. It's a much better solution than a daycare. I cannot be in the house all the time, and I can't take Darcy with me to the fields and barns."

"Of course."

"This way Darcy isn't being shifted around to different people each day. She is here, with me, and with Elli. Isn't it good to have normalcy? I thought a nanny was a far better option."

Elli stood dumbly through the exchange. She knew why he'd said it and it made the best sense. But it stung. It stung a lot. Was being in a relationship such a bad thing? Not that they were, but the way he'd put it sounded so cold.

"A stable environment is definitely one of the things we look for," Angela replied. She gestured toward the table, inviting Elli to take a seat. "And Mr. Black is paying you, Ms. Marchuk?"

Elli swallowed, but schooled her features. If Wyatt could do this, so could she. "Yes, we've agreed on that arrangement."

"Ms. Marchuk, how do you know Mr. Black?"

Elli couldn't look at him. She knew if she did it would seem as though she were looking to him for answers. She sat at the end of the table, perching on the edge of the chair. "We're neighbors. I've lived next door to Wyatt for the last two months, ever since he moved in."

Angela Beck took the chair opposite, leaving Wyatt standing in the doorway. "And you're not romantically involved?"

Elli thought back to the kiss last night, and it was like being there again, feeling Wyatt's hands on her arms and the softness of his lips against her own. But did a kiss signify romantic involvement? On the surface, she supposed it did. But they had backed off and put Darcy first. And he had just called her the nanny in front of the social worker. The nanny. Not "a friend" or even a neighbor. The nanny. That told her quite clearly where Wyatt's feelings stood.

"No, we're not dating." That at least was truthful. Until Darcy's arrival, the sum total of their interaction had been a brief argument in the middle of a pasture. She still refused to look at him, instead seeing the dark blue denim of his jeans in her peripheral vision.

"And how long have you lived next door?"

Elli lifted her chin. "I'm housesitting for family friends at the moment. I was laid off from my job in Calgary and took the offer to stay at their place while I upgrade some courses and look for work."

She really hoped that didn't sound pathetic. Lord knew she wasn't alone. Lots of people had lost their jobs lately as the economy tanked. Surely she couldn't be judged just because she'd been a victim of budget cuts.

"And you're single?"

"Recently divorced."

She could feel Wyatt's gaze on her and she refused to

meet it. She knew if she did she would blush and that would betray her words. She hadn't lied. They weren't dating. But it didn't mean there wasn't an attraction on her part and she did not want to give that away. There was too much at stake.

"Children?"

She swallowed, held Beck's gaze. "No."

"What do you feel qualifies you for this position, then?"

And finally she couldn't help it. Her gaze rose to Wyatt's. His face was nearly unreadable, but she saw a softening around his eyes. He was thinking—as she was—of the baby she'd lost. And he would not say a word about it. She could tell by the compassion in his eyes. Her secret was safe.

She faced Angela again and offered a smile, bolstered by Wyatt's silent support across the room. "I'm available," she began, "and more than that, I have love to give. A baby's needs are simple—food, sleep, diaper changes. Anyone can provide that. What Darcy needs is love and attention and security. I can help Wyatt provide all of that. Most daycares won't even think of taking a newborn. With me here, Darcy is guaranteed to have the undivided attention of at least one of us at all times. She'll have some sort of consistency."

As she finished, a thin cry came from behind her. "And speaking of," Elli continued, trying very hard to smile while keeping a tight grip on her emotions, "I think someone would like her swing wound again. If you'll excuse me?"

"Of course. It is a perfect time for me to begin the interview with Mr. Black."

Darcy was sucking on her hands again, so Elli quickly warmed a bottle and took it with her to the bedroom. "I'll give you some privacy," she murmured to Wyatt as she passed him. "We'll be in the bedroom if you need me."

The softened look around his eyes was gone, replaced by a hard, distrusting edge. He was so afraid, she realized, and wondered why. Everything she'd seen him do the past three days—everything—had been for Darcy's well-being and at sacrifice to his own. Was he hiding something more that she should be concerned about?

"It'll be fine," she reassured him in a low voice. She wanted to reach out and touch him but held back. It wasn't the time or the place, not when she was simply the nanny. Remembering his choice of words made it slightly easier for her to walk away.

Once in the bedroom she arranged the spare pillows on the bed and got comfortable, Darcy cradled in her arms. "Okay, sweet pea," she said softly, adjusting her position and Darcy's weight until both were comfortable. Darcy eagerly took the bottle and Elli sighed. She could hear Wyatt's deep voice and Angela's feminine one from the kitchen. Her back stiffened against the headboard, and she sighed. The sofa would have been more comfortable, but Wyatt needed privacy. Elli thought briefly of the rocking chair she'd bought but Tim had returned to the store, insisting it didn't match their decor.

The solid wood and Quaker design would have fit in here perfectly.

It would have fit in, but she didn't. Even if she had been pretending she did, she realized. Today had shown her that. She was still on the outside, looking in through a dusty pane of glass. This wasn't about her. It was about Wyatt and Darcy and protecting his family. His explanation today that she was "just" the nanny had shown her that he would do what was necessary to keep Darcy with him. That he was sticking to their original arrangement. And of course he should.

But it was very clear that she was not Wyatt's priority despite their pretty little scenes together. If nothing else, the past few days had shown her that dissolving her marriage to Tim had been the right thing. For even if she didn't belong here, she was coming to understand what it was she wanted. And it had nothing to do with a fancy house and expensive car and having the right things.

She wouldn't settle for anything less than it all. Not ever again.

CHAPTER NINE

WYATT COULDN'T AVOID the house any longer. Not the house in particular, but Elli. Darcy was too little to ask questions, of course, but Elli could. And would. She seemed to notice every little thing about him, reading him better than anyone he ever remembered.

It was incredibly disconcerting.

But dark was coming on and he'd relied on her for too long today. Darcy was his responsibility and Elli was here to help. He couldn't hide out in the barns any longer. Chores were long finished. It was time to regroup and move on.

He made it as far as the veranda, with his hand on the handle of the door, but he couldn't make himself go in. Not yet.

Instead he turned, rested his hands on the old wood railing. The veranda faced north, and he gazed out over the brown, empty field across the road. Next year it would provide hay for his herd, and he could almost see the welcoming green-brown grasses, waving in the prairie wind.

This was all he'd ever wanted. A place to call his own. To leave the past behind him. To find his own way, make his own living. He'd done it, too, relying on himself, putting money away until he'd found this place. His Realtor had looked at him skeptically when he'd said he wanted it. It had been neglected and had fallen into disrepair. His herd for this year was small. But the challenge of rebuilding, of growing it into something vital and important was exciting.

Until today, when he'd had to face his past all over again. All the prying, awful queries that he'd had to answer about his upbringing. He had come away from the meeting angry and resentful and afraid, and those were three emotions he'd worked very hard to overcome. He couldn't explain it all to Elli. He needed her on his side in this and if she knew the ugly truth she'd be gone like a shot. Elli was too good, too pure to get wrapped up in his baggage. He'd do well to remember it.

When he thought of her waiting inside, he tensed all over again. She'd looked so pretty today in her red sweater and makeup. He hadn't missed the little touches around the house either, the pillows and tablecloth and, for heaven's sake, matching dishcloths. He scowled. Before Miss Beck had come he'd recognized them as a good idea. But now... this was his house. Elli's presence was everywhere, in every corner. The past forty-eight hours had moved at warp speed and he was struggling to keep up mentally and physically. Coming in to a bunch of feminine touches was simply too much. Something had to give.

"Wyatt?"

He spun, his breath catching in surprise as she appeared as if she'd materialized from his thoughts. The porch light highlighted her pale hair, making her look soft and alluring. "I didn't hear you come out."

"No, you were in another world."

She was right, and it had been a world with her in it, so he didn't answer.

She stepped up beside him, mimicking his stance with her hands on the railing. Her voice was soft, so that it almost seemed part of the breeze. "Do you want to tell me where you were?"

He deliberately misunderstood her. "In the barns."

She laughed lightly, ending on a sigh. "That's not what I meant."

He expected her to go on, but she didn't. She just waited patiently, as if it didn't matter if he said anything more or not. She simply stood beside him, breathing deeply of the crisp autumn air. Her scent, something light and floral, drifted over to him and he felt his muscles tighten in response. This was why he'd stayed away. Because after Angela had departed, he'd wanted nothing more than to seek Elli out. To have her near, to bury his face in her sweet-smelling hair and feel that everything was right again. And that would have been a mistake.

"Where's Darcy?"

"Sleeping. She had a bath and her bottle. She's such a good baby, Wyatt. When you first showed up at my door, I had no idea what I was doing. But Darcy's shown me, bless her."

"You didn't seem unsure. Angela seemed pleased enough with you being Darcy's nanny." Wyatt turned away from the view and rested his hips against the railing so he could look into her face. It was calm, serene even, while he still felt in such turmoil. Again he fought against the urge to pull her into his arms. No, he was stronger than that. He had to keep the lines drawn.

"Nanny." Elli's voice sounded flat. "That certainly tells me where I stand, doesn't it?"

Was she angry with him? She crossed her arms over her chest, chafing them as if she was cold, but even Wyatt understood the defensive body language. "What was I supposed to say, Elli?"

That caused her to pause, and her gaze flew to his.

"What was I supposed to tell her?" he asked. "That I barely knew you? That we were friends?" He swallowed hard. "That I kissed you last night and it was a mistake?"

"Of course not," she whispered. Her eyes had widened as he'd spoken and he regretted the harsh way he'd said it.

"I had to present everything in a positive way for Darcy's sake. And thank God I did. I might lose her anyway now."

Elli's lips dropped open. He could see she was surprised by his last remark, and part of him wanted to confide in her but another part wanted to lock it all away as he'd done for the past fifteen years.

But Elli's response surprised him. "I'm not just a nanny to you, then?"

"Elli…"

"That was our agreement, but I really hated that part, you know. The part where you cozied up to her with your smiles and saying all the right things and passed me off as only the nanny, like some appendage to the situation that could be replaced at a moment's notice if it wasn't convenient."

She reminded him of a little girl who lifted her chin and accepted a dare while being scared to death on the inside. Defiant and terrified. He wondered why. Was she afraid of him? Of herself?

The air hummed between them while he fought for the right thing to say. "Why do we have to quantify our relationship at all? Elli, are you…" He paused, not believing it was true but wanting to know just the same. "Are you *jealous* of Miss Beck?"

A faint blush blossomed on her cheeks.

"You are." By all rights the knowledge should have made

him retreat, away from messy emotions that had no place in this situation. A solid reason to back away, his head was telling him. She'd managed to insinuate herself into nearly every aspect of his life in the past few days, and without even trying.

He should be backing off. But he found himself slightly flattered. Maybe she hadn't been as immune to his kiss last night as he'd thought.

He stepped forward, mysteriously charmed by the roses in her cheeks. He'd thought calling her the nanny was the clearest and best way of defining the situation, especially to someone who had a say in the matter. Angela Beck, for all her pretty looks and smiles, had more power than he was comfortable with. *He* didn't regret kissing *her,* not really. And it sure didn't stop him from wanting to do it again, despite his better judgment.

He was close enough that now she had to tilt her head to look up at him. It would take only the slightest shift and his lips could be on hers. The idea hovered there for a moment, and the way her breath was coming, in shallow, quiet gasps, he could tell she was thinking about it, too.

"It made me feel...pushed to the side," she finally admitted, lowering her chin and breaking the moment. "Marginalized. Like I was...somehow expendable."

That hurt, because making her feel that way was the last thing Wyatt wanted. Couldn't she see that he cared about her? That he was trying to protect her, too? But how could he do that and still protect himself?

"That certainly wasn't how it was meant," he consoled her. "Do you know what it meant to be able to say that today? To be able to point out that Darcy was cared for so well? And you were here, looking after her, and making coffee, and backing me up, showing her that I was right to trust you." He lifted his fingers to her face, touched the cool, soft skin of her cheek. "No one has ever done that for me before. No one. I never meant to make you feel like less because of it, Elli."

He understood her insecurity and refused to add to it by making her feel unimportant. He leaned forward, just enough that their bodies brushed and he lowered his head, his Stetson shadowing them from the light of the porch. Her lips were warm, pliant and just a little bit hesitant. The sweetness fired his blood more than any passionate embrace might have.

"It was just for show. You are more than a nanny, Elli," he murmured against her lips. "But I couldn't let the social worker see that."

Elli stepped out of his embrace. He could see her fingers tremble as she touched her lips and then dropped her hand.

"You trust me?"

"Of course I do. Why do you continue to doubt it? I would only leave Darcy with someone I trusted."

"But you hardly know me!"

His smile followed her as she went back to the railing, putting several feet between them.

"I know you better after two days than I know most people after two years, Ellison."

She shook her head, her face white now. "Don't. Don't say that."

"Why?"

"B-because it...it..." She kept stammering and his heart beat faster, not sure what her answer would be but knowing what he hoped. Nothing could have surprised him more, but there it was.

"Because it scares you?"

"Yes," she whispered.

The air began to hum again.

Elli blinked, swallowed. He watched each movement with great attention, trying to drink in every nuance of her. She had lost so much over the past months. Wyatt had overcome many of his demons through the years, but Elli's wounds were fresh. Surely, for this once, he could say what he felt if it meant giving her back some of her self-esteem.

"Angela Beck is no more beautiful than you, Elli."

"You're just trying to distract me." Her eyes narrowed. "My hair was a mess and any fool can see I am overweight and...well, she looked so put together and perfect!"

Was that what this was about? Perfection? He'd learned long ago that perfection was overrated and impossible. It was intimidating and unsustainable, as well. "What you are, Ellison Marchuk, is *real*."

He closed the distance between them once more, this time leaving her no escape as his body blocked her from the front and the railing from the back. He put his hands on her waist and drew her closer so that their bodies brushed. His fingers trailed over her ribs and down the curve of her hip. "I don't want you to be perfect. I want you to be just as you are. I like your curves, and the way your hair curls around your forehead, and just about everything about you."

"Oh, Wyatt," she whispered, and he could tell she was tempted to give in.

Elli heard the words and felt his hands slide over the pockets of her pants. She sighed, a sound of bliss and longing and fear. Did he really mean it? When was the last time someone had taken her as she was and it had actually been okay? Everyone always expected more of her.

She should be smarter, more ambitious, neater, prettier, thinner. And yet Wyatt didn't seem to care about any of that. At the same time she wanted to be more *for* him. He was a good man, she could tell. Strong and honorable and gorgeous without even trying.

His hand rested at her waist as his voice touched her, deep and sad. "Whoever told you otherwise isn't here now, Elli. Let it go."

Oh, the kindness was nearly too much to bear. If he kept on, she'd start crying and that would be a horrible mess. The only way to hold it together was to straighten her spine and dismiss his kindness. All of it, and keep only the sweet memory of his words locked inside like a treasure.

"Let it go like I suppose you have, Wyatt?"

She nearly cringed at how harsh her words sounded. Was she so wrapped up in protecting herself that she'd hurt him to do it? Shame burned within her. His hand stopped moving on her hip and she felt him straighten, the intimate moment lost.

"I don't know what you mean." He dismissed her comment, but she knew he was lying. She'd fought back simply to avoid being pulled down into more sadness, but his evasive answer somehow made her mad. She had been rude, but it had also been an honest question. He could see into her so easily—why shouldn't she know more about him? She wanted him to be straight with her. She needed it.

"You know exactly what I mean. You hightailed it out of here after Angela left and hid out in the barns ever since. That had nothing to do with me. What did you mean before, that you might lose her anyway?"

"It doesn't matter now," he replied, backing away. He turned and headed toward the veranda steps.

Elli watched him walk away, and anger warred with remorse for turning the tables on him. She'd thought she wanted to hear him confirm that yes, she was simply there to help Darcy. It would have made it much easier to fight her growing attraction, knowing it wasn't returned. But he hadn't. He'd brought up the kiss, the one she couldn't erase from her mind. And then he'd kissed her again, making her toes curl. Why had he done it? Because he meant it? Every cell in her body wanted to believe that, but a nagging voice in her head told her it was merely a method to distract her from the real issue—the reason he'd disappeared after Miss Beck had departed.

Now he was shutting her out and walking away when she was aching to understand why a mere mention of his interview made his face turn pale and his shoulders stiffen. What had happened to make him seek solitude for hours? Why was he hurting so much?

"Never took you for a runner, Black," she accused, heart in her throat. She deliberately provoked him, knowing that if she went the gentle route he'd simply dismiss her.

Her sharp words had the desired effect. He turned back and his eyes blazed at her. "You don't know what you're talking about."

"No, I don't. But I figure it's something big when it makes you leave the house and hide out in the barns. When you spend hours alone rather than face us in the house. When you miss dinner and bath time with Darcy and choose to spend the evening in an unheated barn. And it's got to be really something if you attempt to distract me by kissing me. I asked a simple question and you ran away."

"It's nothing." He started to turn away again, guilt written all over his face.

"No, it's not. It's a whole lot of something, and I know fear when I see it. If I'm staying here, if Darcy is staying here…" She paused, afraid to speak her mind, but wanting to be stronger than she'd ever been before. "If we're starting something, I think I deserve to know."

He spun on her so quickly she could react only by stepping backward. "I don't owe you anything," he growled.

"And if we want to talk about running, what exactly are you doing, Elli? I'm not blind. What are you doing at the Camerons' if not hiding away from life, huh? Running, hiding...we all have something, don't we?" He scoffed. "What are you doing here anyway? Playing at reality? You and your tablecloths and doilies and God knows what else."

Elli recoiled inside as the harsh words sliced into her, but she held her ground and lifted her chin. He would not intimidate her, even if he was one hundred percent right. She knew what pain looked like; she'd seen it in the mirror for months, and now she saw it in the hard planes of his face. They weren't so different in that way. Wyatt was simply afraid. Of what? What could be so bad that he'd fear Darcy was going to be taken away from him?

"I certainly didn't mean to overstep," she said stiffly. "I thought you wanted me to do those things. If you don't like them, I'll put them away and you can keep things just as you want them. And for the record, Wyatt Black, you don't owe me." She had taken Tim's insults, but those days were gone. She was stronger than that now. "Except not to play games." She slid her hands into her pockets, attempting to keep them warm. The evening suddenly seemed much colder. "If what happened just now between us was a game, it was very cruel of you, Wyatt."

His lips dropped open for a moment before he shut them again, forming a firm line. His hat shadowed his eyes, but she could feel the apology in his gaze.

"Oh God, I'm sorry. I don't play games, Elli. I never should have said that."

She knew in her heart he was being honest. Which meant what he'd said was true, and she tried to keep her pulse from spinning out of control. Lord, everything about him was so intense. What would it be like to be loved by a man like Wyatt Black?

"I know," she acquiesced.

His lips relaxed and his shoulders dropped. "I do owe you for all you've done. But not this. Please don't ask me this," he breathed.

Elli sighed, touched by the anguish in his voice. What was she doing? She could feel herself falling. Any plans and decisions she'd made about her future seemed to fly out of her head when he was around. Wyatt was *dangerous*. And it was *exciting*.

Sympathy and provocation hadn't worked. Maybe he had a right to his own secrets. "I'm going back inside, then. There's dinner in the fridge if you want to heat it up."

What an idiot she was, letting herself have feelings for Wyatt, giving in to the intense attraction that seemed to grow with each minute they spent together. He couldn't give her what she needed. He had too many things pulling at his time. Whatever else was between them was only muddying the waters.

Nothing surprised her more than the sound of the door as it creaked open, then clicked shut behind her.

She turned to see him standing in the doorway, his jaw set and his hair slightly messed as if he'd run his hands through it. His hat drooped negligently from his hand. "I am not a runner," he said firmly. "Not anymore."

"Then why did you take off? I came out from feeding Darcy and you were gone. I didn't know where until it got darker and I saw the lights in the barn."

He stepped forward, his eyes pleading with hers, as if they were begging her to understand. "Do you know the kinds of questions she asked, Elli? We're not talking generalities here. Every single last thing you'd rather not talk about? That's what they ask."

He tossed his hat onto a chair and covered his face with his hands.

The gesture was so sudden, so despairing, Elli was at a loss as to what to do. She felt his pain keenly, as piercing as a cold knife, the hopelessness of it. He exhaled slowly and pulled his hands away from his face. She almost wished he hadn't. His eyes were bleak, his cheekbones etched with agony. He looked the way she'd felt the morning she'd awakened and truly realized that William was not going to be in her arms ever again.

"Don't," she said, shaking her head. "I'm sorry I pushed. Don't say it, Wyatt, if it hurts too much. It doesn't matter."

But now he ignored her, as if he'd opened the door and couldn't help but walk through it. "She poked and prodded and pried for every detail you can imagine about any topic you can come up with. That interview invades every single aspect of your life. Perhaps now you can understand why I had to be alone."

"Did she ask about your relationship to Barbara?"

He snorted, a harsh, hurtful sound. "Top of the list. When did I find out she was my sister. Why did I want to look after her child when we barely knew each other. The fact that Barbara was the product of an affair started the probe into our family life."

Elli blanched. Of course. Digging around in painful events would make anyone want to turtle into themselves. "About being taken away? Your father's abuse?"

"Oh, yes." His hands fidgeted and he shoved them in the back pockets of his jeans. His eyes were wild now, like a cornered animal. "My father, that paragon of parenthood, and whether or not I'm cut from the same cloth. Do I solve things with physical violence. What are my thoughts on discipline."

"I'm so sorry, Wyatt."

He took several breaths before responding. "All the things I never wanted to talk about with another living soul. All the demons I've tried to outrun. That's what it was. So I could somehow prove myself worthy."

Elli felt tears sting the backs of her eyes. She understood that the last thing Wyatt would want was to be compared to his father. He was so gentle and caring with Darcy, so dedicated and determined to do the right thing. To insinuate otherwise would cut him to the bone. What if she'd been faced with the same interrogation? Would she have passed? Would she have been able to talk about all her mistakes?

Now she looked at him and saw him swipe at his eyes. Compassion overruled every bit of self-preservation she possessed and she rushed forward to take his hands. "Oh, Wyatt, I'm so sorry," she repeated, not knowing what else to say. "What can I do?"

He led her by the hand to an old battered wing chair. The light from the kitchen highlighted his sharp features as he sat, then tugged her down onto his lap. "Just let me hold you," he murmured, and she felt her heart quake as his arms came around her.

Mentally she'd been trying to push him away for hours. But it felt so good to be held. When William died Tim had pushed her away, pretending everything was all right, denying her the physical touches that might have given some comfort. She was beginning to see that Wyatt, with all his baggage and secrets and sometimes prickly exterior, was far more giving than Tim had ever been and yet he had more reason to hide. She curled into his embrace and tangled her fingers through the dark strands of his hair, wanting to give back to him just a little bit.

"I can do that," she whispered, and for long minutes they sat that way, absorbing strength from each other.

And somehow without meaning it to happen, Elli felt a corner of her heart start to heal.

"Do you know what the saving grace is in all of this?" Wyatt's soft, deep voice finally broke the silence.

"Hmm?" she asked, her eyes closed as she memorized the shape and feel of him, the scent, the way his chest rumbled when he spoke.

"My mother. When I think of Barbara, I think of my mother. Mom would not have turned Barbara away, even though she would have been a reminder of my father's infidelity," he said. His arms tightened ever so slightly. "My mother was kind and generous, and had every reason to be bitter. But she wasn't. The only way I've gotten through this at all is thinking about her. If I was cursed with one parent, I was blessed with the other. I've always tried to be more like her...even if I do look like him."

Of course, Elli realized. What must it be like for Wyatt to resemble someone who had betrayed the very nature of fatherhood? Of course he would want to emulate his mother. "What was she like?"

She felt his facial muscles move as he smiled. "She could do anything. Cook, sew, sing...not that my father gave her much to sing about. But she did it when he was away. She always tried to make things special for me, and she seemed to apologize when she couldn't."

"Why did she stay? Why didn't she take you and leave, Wyatt?"

His response was typical and sad. "Where would she have gone? She was afraid he would find her. Or that he would try to take me. Not that he really wanted me. It was about possession with my father."

She was starting to understand why all the prying questions had affected him so deeply today. "This all came out this afternoon?"

He nodded. "I will not be like my father, Elli."

"Of course not." She straightened and cupped his chin, tilting his face up so she could look him in the eyes. "And you're not. Looking after Darcy isn't about possession for you. I know that. It's about family, and acceptance, and responsibility."

"You see that. But I'm not sure Angela Beck did. It isn't so pretty when it's in black and white."

"What happened to your parents, Wyatt?"

His gaze was steady on hers. "I was working in Fort McMurray. They'd been traveling together and my father had been drinking. The crash killed them both instantly."

She let the news sink in, knowing there was nothing she could say that would be more than a useless platitude. And after today's interview Wyatt was afraid he was going to lose Darcy, too. Darcy and Barbara were the only family he had left. He was determined to look after them both, she could tell. What would happen to Wyatt if he failed?

He couldn't fail. She was here to help ensure it.

"They need to be sure, that's all. They are putting Darcy first, just like you are. They'll see that you're the right person to care for her until Barbara is well again."

"It doesn't make it easier," he replied, calmer now. "So now maybe you understand why I called you the nanny today. I can't let them all down. They're all the family I have left. That's why I can't jeopardize the situation by keeping on like we have been."

She slid off his lap, took the chair opposite him and put her hands on her knees. "What do you mean?"

Wyatt's gaze was apologetic as he leaned forward, resting his forearms on his knees and linking his hands. "I know I said that you were more than just the nanny, but do you think today's visit is the end of it? What if Beck comes back and finds us like we were tonight?"

"We were hardly doing anything wrong," she replied, feeling a sudden chill on her shoulders now that his arms were not about her anymore.

"Maybe not, but how would it look to her? I insisted you are the nanny. I made it clear we're not in a personal relationship. You heard what she said. People cohabiting need to be in a relationship for at least a year, and we've known each other only days. I told her there was nothing romantic between us. If we continue on this way it means I've *lied.* And I simply can't risk it. Darcy is too important to me."

A part of her ached as he said it. She had enjoyed being held by him so much. But Darcy had to come first, and they both knew it. Tonight, she had only fooled herself into thinking she was important to him. And perhaps she was, but she was way down on the list. The new life she wanted to build wasn't here. She'd left the old dreams behind. Wyatt and Darcy were sidetracking her, and at times most pleasantly. Tonight she'd forgotten all her self-promises the moment he'd put his lips on hers. But she had to keep her eye on the big picture.

"Elli...I'm sorry. Sorry I've dragged you into this."

Her heart tugged, hearing him say her name that way. But her resolve was stronger, especially now that he wasn't touching her. She wouldn't let him see he had the power to hurt her. "No, Wyatt. I'm here of my own choosing. You're right. If she got the wrong impression, you could lose Darcy, and I know how much that would eat away at you. You have to do what's best for Darcy."

He nodded. "She's the most important thing now. And lying about our involvement would be a mistake I don't want on my conscience." His eyes were sober, and she thought perhaps held a glint of resentment. "Lies have a way of coming out sooner or later."

She thought of his father denying his own daughter and leaving Barbara's mother to fend for herself. She thought about all that she hadn't told Wyatt about William and felt a niggle of guilt. She hadn't exactly lied, but she hadn't told him the whole truth either. She wasn't sure she ever could.

"You are not your father, Wyatt. You always do the right thing."

The truth was bittersweet. The right thing was costing her. Just when she was starting to feel alive again, she was cruelly reminded of her own unimportance.

A thin cry sounded from the bedroom; Darcy was awake once more.

"So we keep it simple," she said, pushing on her knees and rising from the chair.

"Simple," he echoed.

Elli left him sitting in the dark and went to get Darcy. As she picked her up, warm and nuzzly from sleep, she realized that nothing about their relationship would ever be simple. Not after tonight.

CHAPTER TEN

THE DAYS THAT FOLLOWED set a pattern, and Wyatt was true to their agreement. He was always pleasant and friendly, but there was no more talk of pasts and fathers or any other hot-button topics. Elli cooked meals, cared for Darcy and finished up accounting assignments, e-mailing them to her supervisor. Wyatt asked her quietly to leave the things she'd bought, but there were no more shopping trips to the home décor shop. The fall air turned colder and the leaves scattered from the trees, leaving a golden carpet on the grass. Wyatt cared for his stock, spent hours outside making repairs and moving the herd to different pastures. When he came in his smiles and touches were for Darcy.

As Darcy watched from her swing, Elli washed up the breakfast dishes and put them away in the cozy kitchen. Elli wasn't jealous. It was impossible to be jealous of Darcy, who was an absolute darling. But she found herself wishing that Wyatt could spare a few soft words and gentle touches for her. She missed him. She'd had a taste and she wanted more. Seeing him work so hard and lavish his affection on his niece only made him more amazing in her eyes. She'd promised herself never to settle again, but as she got to know Wyatt even more, she saw so many qualities she admired, wished for in a partner. Stability. Tenderness. Patience. Love.

She was falling in love with him, sure as spring rain.

But the way he'd put on the brakes and then slipped into their daily and functional existence so easily told her that the feeling wasn't reciprocated. Her hands paused on the handle of a cupboard door. Those first days together had been so intense. Emotions had run high and things had been in flux. Now things had settled into a routine. Whatever her feelings for Wyatt, they weren't returned, she was sure of it.

She should be relieved, she supposed. Soon Barbara would be out of the hospital and the Camerons would be back. Elli had to start thinking about what she was going to do next. She told herself that because her feelings were one-sided, there would be fewer complications when it came time to move on.

As she passed Darcy, she reached out and gave the tiny cotton-covered toes a squeeze. It was going to be difficult to see Darcy leave, too, but she'd always known she would. Wyatt would not be a part of Elli's life after that happened and that wouldn't change even if she wished it to. No, she needed to start looking for a job and a place to live as soon as she finished her course.

She heard Wyatt's boots on the veranda and checked the clock on the microwave. Right on time. The past few days he'd come in at precisely ten o'clock for a cup of coffee and a sweet. He did have a sweet tooth and she was more than happy to oblige. She'd enjoyed the looking after Darcy, and Wyatt's house, and cooking meals for more than herself. As the screen door slapped against the frame, she cautioned herself not to get too accustomed to it. She was going to be hurt enough when this was over; forming habits would not help.

Wyatt stood in the doorway, grinning as if he was holding some sort of secret, looking unexpectedly youthful. The lines that had crinkled the corners of his eyes were gone, and there was an air of hopefulness about him.

She couldn't help the smile that curved her lips in return. He looked so pleased with himself, his dark eyes alight with some mischief and his hair even more windblown than usual. He held his hat in his hands, and she noticed he was crumpling the sides.

"What are you up to? And I know it's not my banana bread making you smile that way."

He made a show of sniffing the air. "You're right, although now that you mention it, it does smell good in here."

"It's just out of the oven and too hot to slice, so stay away from that cooling rack." She struggled to keep her lips stern as she brandished a mixing spoon, but felt the corner of her mouth quiver. What was it about him that made her smile so easily? He looked like a boy with a new toy.

He came across the kitchen and tipped a finger at Darcy's nose. "I have a surprise for you both."

"A surprise?" Elli folded the tea towel in her hands and draped it over the handle of the oven door. Curiosity got the better of her and she couldn't resist asking, "What kind of surprise?"

"Just something I've been working on the last week or so."

Elli's mind whirred. The past week—that would be ever since the night they'd agreed to keep things platonic and he'd started spending more time in the fields and barns. What could he possibly have to surprise them with?

"Stay here, okay? I've got to bring it in."

She wanted to refuse but couldn't, not at the hopeful look he sent her before he spun and disappeared out the door.

She heard an odd clunking as he came back. "Close your

eyes!" he called out from the porch, and she did, anticipation causing a quiver in her tummy. No one had surprised her in a very long time.

"Are they closed?" More clunking and thunking came from the entry.

Elli giggled. "Yes, they're closed. But hurry up!"

Some shuffling and scraping and then Wyatt came back to the kitchen. "Bring Darcy," he said, and Elli could see he was practically bouncing on the balls of his feet. His Stetson was pushed back on his head, making him look even more young and boyish and very, very attractive.

She picked Darcy up out of her swing and said, "Okay. Lead on before you burst."

He led the way into the living room. "What do you think?"

In the corner where the makeshift table had been now sat the most beautiful rocking chair Elli had ever seen. Stunningly simple, with a curved seat and perfect spindles along the back, painstakingly sanded and stained a beautiful rich oak. On the seat was a flowered cushion in blues and pinks.

A lump rose in her throat as she tried to think of the words to say. "It's beautiful, Wyatt," she murmured, holding tight to Darcy.

"I found it in the back shed, of all places," Wyatt explained. He went to the chair and stood behind it, resting his hands on the back. "It was dirty and scratched, but it just needed some love. Some fine grit sanding and a few coats of stain."

He had done this himself? With his hands? Somehow it meant much more knowing he hadn't just gone to a store and picked it out. It almost felt…like a lover's gift. But that was silly, wasn't it? Who gave a lover a rocking chair?

There was also the small matter of things being strictly friendly between them lately.

It felt intimate just the same.

"You did this?" The words came through her lips tight and strained. She tried to smile encouragingly to cover.

"It was a bit of a shock at first, you know," he said, undaunted by her cool response. "When I came in and saw all the...well, the feminine touches around the place. I've been a bachelor a long time, Elli, but you didn't deserve the criticism I doled out. And you know, I've gotten used to it." His eyes danced at her. "Now I even like it. I wanted to make it up to you and didn't know how. Then there it was and I realized you need a proper chair. Come and sit in it with Darcy."

Elli's knees shook now as she walked across the room. She hadn't meant to make Wyatt uncomfortable in his own home, and his apology had made things right. He didn't need to do this. She was touched.

"I didn't mean to overstep," she whispered.

"You didn't. You just had the sense to do what I wouldn't do for myself. Come on," he cajoled, giving the chair a little rock. "I've tried it. It's stable, I promise."

For days she'd lamented a comfortable seating arrangement for feeding the baby or for soothing her as she fussed. She'd remembered the chair she'd bought and returned while expecting William, and wished she had something similar, especially when Darcy seemed particularly difficult to soothe and Elli's back ached from leaning against the headboard of Wyatt's bed. But her reaction now was immediate and frightening. Grief and longing hovered on the edge of her heart as she was faced with the actual object rather than the thought. She inhaled deeply, struggling for control. How could she refuse to sit in it when Wyatt was looking so pleased with himself? And he deserved to be.

She could do this. She could stay in control. She sat tentatively on the seat, the weight of Darcy in her arms awkward in a way it hadn't been since the very first day. Her shoulders tensed as she leaned against the back. "It's wonderful, Wyatt. Thank you."

But he'd gone quiet behind her, as if he'd sensed something wasn't quite right. "You're tense," he observed, and his hands settled on her shoulders. "What's wrong?" His fingers kneaded gently, trying to work out the knots that had formed. And as he moved his hands, the chair began to rock.

Elli looked down into Darcy's contented face, saw the blue eyes looking up at her, unfocused, the tiny, perfectly shaped lips, and in the breath of a moment her control slipped and everything blurred.

Once the tears started, Elli couldn't make them stop. The chair tipped forward and back but each movement pushed the tears closer to the edge of her lashes until the first ones slid down her cheeks. She caught her breath on a little hiccup, trying desperately to get a grip on her emotions.

But the memory was so utterly real that she lost the battle.

"Elli...my God, what is it?" Wyatt came around from behind the chair and knelt before her. He swept the Stetson from his head and put it on the couch beside them. Her heart gave a lurch at the action, gentle and gallant. His face loomed before hers, his eyes shadowed with concern. She did love him. There was no way she could have avoided it. Knowing it was one-sided, on top of the pain already slicing into her, only increased the despair cresting over her.

"It's just...just that..." She gasped for breath and felt another sob building. "The last time I rocked...it was..."

But she couldn't finish. Her mouth worked but no words

came out. Only an oddly high, keening sound as she sat in the chair he'd made for her and finally fully, grieved for the son she'd lost.

It had been William in her arms, her son, unbearably small but perfectly formed, painstakingly bathed by the nurses and swaddled in the white-and-blue flannel of the hospital. No breath passed his lips; his lashes lay in rest on his pale cheeks. But she had held him close and rocked him and said goodbye.

Wyatt reached for Darcy, but Elli held on unreasonably, turning her arm away from Wyatt's prying hands. "No! Don't take him yet. You can't take him yet."

Then her ears registered what she'd said and she broke down completely with shame and grief. Wyatt took Darcy gently from her now unresisting arms and laid her on the play mat on the floor.

When he returned, he simply bent and lifted Elli out of the chair, an arm around her back and the other beneath her knees, lifting her as if she weighed nothing. She clung to his hard, strong body, putting her arms around his neck and pressing her forehead against it. He went to the sofa and sat, holding her in his lap. "Let it out," he whispered against her hair, and she felt him kiss the top of her head. "For God's sake, Elli, let it out."

She did, all the while clinging to his neck as the pain and anger and grief finally let loose. This was what she'd held in for months, trying to keep up appearances, determined to show the world she could function. It had been building all this time, brought to the surface by loving Darcy as she cared for her, and now spilled over by loving Wyatt, by trusting him.

And she did trust him. Even if he never returned her love, she knew she trusted him completely. In all her life she'd never known a better man. Gradually her breaths slowed, grew regular, and exhaustion and relief made her limbs limp and relaxed. He felt good, solid. Tim had scoffed at her tears, turning her away. Perhaps that had been his way of handling the grief—by not showing it at all—and she'd been forced to hold it in, too. With Wyatt there was no pretending. She could be who she had to be.

"I didn't know," Wyatt said softly, once she was in firm control. His hand rubbed over her upper arm, soothing and warm. "How long have you been holding that in?"

Elli sighed, her eyes still closed so she could focus on the feel of him, warm and firm, the way his fingers felt through the fabric of her sweater. "Thirteen months."

Over a year. William had been gone over a year and she suddenly knew she was no closer to being over it than she'd been then. She'd only gone through the motions.

Darcy lay on the floor, looking up at the colors and shapes of the baby gym above her. Watching her caused a bittersweet ache to spread through Elli's chest. She missed the opportunities most. The opportunity to see her son grow, change, to be able to love him and see the light of recognition in his eyes at the sound of her voice or the touch of her hands.

"I had been waiting so long to have my baby," she confessed, finally giving words to the pain. "I never had the chance to learn with him. To feed him or change him or rock him to sleep. I imagined what it would be like for months, but theory is different than practice." She tried to smile, but it wobbled. "And then you showed up with Darcy...." Her voice trailed off, uncertain.

He lifted his head and looked at her face. Oh, she knew she looked dreadful. She rushed to wipe at her cheeks, to smooth her messed hair. But Wyatt didn't seem to care about her appearance. He never had. He raised his left hand and wiped away the moisture beneath her eyes with the pad of his thumb.

He touched her cheek softly, cupping her jaw lightly in his hand and applying gentle pressure so she would turn her face toward him. "It was a boy," he said, and she remembered what she'd blurted out in the chair.

For a moment it had been as if she was back in the hospital with William instead of there in the living room with Darcy.

Wyatt kept a firm hold on his emotions. There was more going on with Elli than he had ever dreamed and somehow the chair had set her off. He'd done the only thing he could—held her until the storm was over. She tried to turn away, but he kept his fingers firm on her face. "Elli?"

"Yes, he was a boy," she whispered, and he caught the glimmer of remnant tears in the corners of her eyes. Her teeth worried her lower lip.

And if she knew it was a boy, it meant she'd carried him long enough to know. How long? Months, certainly. He couldn't comprehend what that must be like, to carry a life and then just…not. He thought she'd told him that she had miscarried. But it didn't add up, not now. When a person thought of miscarriage, they thought of pregnancies ended in the early stages, the first few months. To know her baby was a boy, and the rocking chair today… It didn't take much effort to connect the dots.

"You were further along in your pregnancy than you let me believe, weren't you?" He said it gently, urging her to talk. She clearly needed to. And he wanted to listen. Not because he felt obligated in any way but because there was something about Elli that reached inside him. He couldn't explain it, or quantify what or why. He just wanted to. He wanted to help her the way she'd helped him.

"I was six weeks to term," she murmured, and the tears

that had been sitting in the corners of her eyes slid silently down her cheeks. "My water broke and I knew it was too early. It should have been okay. We just thought he'd be small, and spend some time in the neonatal unit."

It took her a few seconds to collect herself. "There was an additional problem with his lungs we hadn't known about, a defect. I…"

She stopped, lowered her head.

"You don't have to say it," he said gently, feeling his heart quake for her. He'd been hiding out in the barns and thinking only of himself, first to escape the false domesticity she was providing and then thinking how proud he'd be to present her with that stupid chair to make up for hurting her feelings. He'd thought about making it easier for her to care for Darcy, and a way to say thank-you, since she had yet to cash the check he had written. It had hurt, brushing her aside and insisting they keep things platonic. If circumstances were different, he would have pursued her.

She was the first person he'd willingly told about his past, and it hadn't been easy. But his pain was nothing compared to hers. His loss was nothing when held up to the loss of a child.

She carried on, even though he could barely hear the whispered words. "I never got to hear him cry."

There was a plaintive plea in her words and he tightened his arms around her. "I'm so sorry."

"I thought I was over it more than this," she whispered. She wasn't fighting his embrace, and he settled more deeply into the cushions. Her weight felt good on his lap, holding her the way he'd wanted to for days. Just being close to her, connected, felt right.

"Sometimes it takes people years to really grieve." He sighed, knowing how long it had taken him to accept that his mother was truly gone. It had been just recently that he'd made peace with it. And only then that he'd been able to sort out his life and know what he really wanted. This ranch was that resolution put into action. A testament to his mother's faith in him and finally his faith in himself.

"Back in Calgary, everyone kept asking how I was doing. I could never answer them honestly. I had to put on a smile and give them some stock response."

"And your husband?"

"Grief either brings you together or drives you apart. Our relationship didn't have the right foundation, and it didn't weather the stress of it. Tim buried himself in work and I…"

When she paused, Wyatt gave her hand a squeeze. She was being brave, though he doubted she knew it.

"I built myself a shell."

Wyatt smiled. "Oh, I can relate to that, all right."

And finally, a smile in return, with puffy lips and red-rimmed eyes. "I guess you probably can." Then the smile faded.

"Ain't life something?" Wyatt shrugged. "I realized a while back that it's not the disaster that defines a person, Elli. It's what you do afterward that counts."

"And I haven't done anything." Her eyebrows drew together. "I've just put it all off."

"There's always today. Today's a good day to make a new start."

Wyatt knew what he wanted her to say. That this platonic relationship was a waste of time. That she would make a new start with him once Darcy went home. Barbara's doctors reported she was doing well and soon Darcy would be going home. There wouldn't be a social worker standing in their way.

"I'm not sure I'm quite ready for that yet. I just…oh." Her voice caught again. "I miss him," she said simply.

"No one said you had to do it overnight," he replied, disappointed. "But making a start—and getting it all out, if that's what it takes—is good."

"You're a good man, Wyatt Black."

She cupped his face in her hands and he felt her blue gaze penetrate. Even with the evidence of crying marring her face, he could honestly say he wanted her, more than he'd ever wanted a woman. It was deeper than a simple physical need. His gaze dropped to her lips and back up again and he saw acknowledgment in her eyes. "Not as good as you think," he murmured. His resolution was forgotten when faced with her sweet vulnerability.

Her fingers still framed his face and he leaned forward, needing to touch her, taste her, wanting to somehow make things right for her in the only way he knew how.

He put his lips over hers and kissed her softly, wanting to convince her to open up to him that little bit more. For a few seconds she seemed to hold her breath, and the moment paused, like standing on a ledge of indecision.

But then she relaxed, melting into him, curling into his body as her mouth softened, warm and pliable beneath his. As his body responded, he wondered how in hell any man in his right mind could have let her go.

Elli heard the small sound of acquiescence that escaped her throat as Wyatt took control of the kiss. Oh, his body felt so hard, so reassuring. He knew everything now and he wasn't running, he wasn't changing the subject. He was a man in a million, and he was kissing her as if she was the most cherished woman on the planet.

She melted against him, letting him fold her in his arms as he shifted his weight on the sofa. Want, desire such as she hadn't felt in months slid seductively through her veins.

His body pressed her into the cushions and she welcomed

the weight, feeling at once wanted and protected. As his
mouth left hers and pressed kisses to her cheeks, down the
sweep of her jaw, she suddenly understood that she wasn't
cold, or standoffish, or any of the things Tim had accused
her of. She had simply been waiting. Waiting for the right
person to come along and set her free.

And she was. As Wyatt's mouth returned to hers, she
slid her hands over his hips and up beneath his shirt, feeling the warm skin beneath the cotton.

His hips pressed against her and her blood surged.

"Elli…"

"Shhh," she replied, touching her lips to his neck and
feeling his pulse pounding there. She licked along the rough
skin, tasting, feeling pleasure not only in what he was doing
to her but from knowing what she was doing to him. After
months of feeling powerless, it was liberating, affirming,
and she craved more.

Wyatt pushed against the arm of the sofa with his hands
so that he was looking down into her face. Elli noted with
satisfaction that his breath came in ragged gasps and his
lips were puffed from kissing.

"I definitely need a new couch," he murmured, his voice
a soft growl. "Not here. My bed."

Taking it to the bedroom was a logical next step and one
Elli thought she was ready for, but a thread of nervousness
nagged. "But Darcy…"

"Has fallen asleep on her play mat."

He looked into her eyes, took one hand and slid it over
the curve of her breast.

It was almost impossible to think when he was touching her like that, and thinking was starting to sound quite
overrated.

She ran her hand over the back pocket of his jeans and
offered the challenge with her eyes.

In a quick move Wyatt was off her, and she felt the lack of him immediately. It was quickly replaced by exhilaration as he scooped her off the sofa and carried her down the hall to the bedroom. Once inside, he laid her on the bed, sat beside her and began unbuttoning his shirt.

Elli's heart slammed against her ribs. A slice of well-muscled chest showed as his shirt gaped open, and she wanted to touch it. She wanted him, but modesty fought to be heard. What would he say when he saw her body? She fought against her insecurities, trying to ignore the hurtful comments in her memory. He hadn't turned away yet. She had to believe he wouldn't now.

She swallowed as she knelt on the mattress and pulled her sweater over her head.

Wyatt was there in the breath of a moment, kneeling before her, pulling her forward so her skin was pressed against his. She thrilled to touch it, to feel the heat and strength of it against her. She reached to push his shirt off his shoulders.

And then they both heard it—a knock on the front door.

For a split second they froze, then Wyatt jumped off the bed and went to the window.

"It's Angela Beck."

"Oh, my God!"

The seriousness of the situation hit them both and Elli scrambled for her sweater as the knock sounded again. "You've got to answer the door!" she whispered loudly. "Go, Wyatt!"

He was already buttoning his shirt. "You're already dressed."

"Yes, but look at me!" She tried to keep the panic out of her voice, but didn't succeed very well. What had they been thinking, getting carried away? "My eyes are blotchy and my hair's a disaster!"

"All right. Take a moment to collect yourself." He gave her arm a quick squeeze. "It'll be fine."

But the worried look in his eyes belied his reassurances.

This was her fault. He had been clear about keeping things platonic and why. She should have stopped him at the first kiss. He hadn't put her first, and so she had done it for him. And now what a mess they were in!

Elli scrambled to tuck her hair into a ponytail as she heard Wyatt answer the door. She should have stopped him, but she hadn't wanted to. If they hadn't been interrupted, she would have made love with him.

And now, with the faint sound of Angela Beck's voice coming from the other end of the house, the insanity of it grabbed her. She wasn't sure how she was going to walk out there and pretend everything was normal, not when she could still feel his body against hers and taste him on her lips.

And beneath it all was a nagging fear. Would he blame her if today's visit went wrong?

CHAPTER ELEVEN

WHEN ELLI ENTERED the kitchen, Angela Beck was seated at the table with a cup of coffee and Wyatt was calmly slicing through the banana bread. She exhaled slowly, thankful he'd been able to collect himself so quickly, giving her time to regroup. Fixing her hair, a reviving splash of cold water on her face and a good foundation had done its work, she hoped.

"Ellison!" Angela turned in her chair as Elli stepped forward. "I'm glad you're here. I stopped by to check on Darcy, of course, and give Wyatt an update."

Elli stole a glance at Wyatt, wondering what he'd offered for an explanation and afraid to respond lest she contradict anything he may have said. "Darcy's doing well. She really is a good baby."

"Yes, I saw her sleeping on her mat."

Darcy at least was a safe topic. "We put her down to play, and she just drifted off."

Wyatt broke in to the exchange as he put a plate of banana bread on the table. "Did you get your assignment sent, Elli?"

Elli took her cue and hoped to heaven she wasn't blushing. "Yes, I did, thank you. Only two more to go."

Wyatt smiled easily at Angela. "Elli is taking accounting courses online."

The conversation went well for several minutes as they sat and had coffee and sweets and talked about Darcy. Angela's face turned serious, though, when she began to speak with them about Barbara.

"The good news is, Barbara is making excellent progress. Her doctors are very pleased, as I'm sure you're aware."

Wyatt nodded. Elli knew he'd spoken to his sister's physician a few days earlier and had been encouraged.

"We do want to place Darcy back with her mom as soon as we can. As a mother, she needs to spend time with her baby, to develop that important bond. From our side, we need to ensure that the baby is in a safe, secure and loving environment."

"What does this all mean?" Elli asked, the banana bread suddenly dry in her mouth. Would this go on longer than planned, or shorter? And which did she want? The idea of staying here with Wyatt, especially after this morning, was heady. But scary, too. They'd nearly been caught, and she knew Wyatt would blame himself if Darcy went into foster care even for a short time simply because he'd fudged the truth about their relationship. The other option was that he'd be even more determined to keep their relationship businesslike, an arrangement that didn't suit her at all. Then of course, there was the chance that Barbara would be out of hospital quickly and Elli wouldn't have a reason to stay.

"It means that your situation here is hopefully going to resolve very soon. It also means that Barbara is going to need a lot of support. Because she went to the hospital, she'll get the help she needs. Her doctor will be monitoring her health, as will child and family services. Really, going for help was the best thing Barbara could have done. She'll have access to many resources to help her through this, some mandated and some not, including support groups."

"And family," Wyatt replied, folding his hands on the table before him. "I'm her brother. I'll be there, as well."

Angela smiled. "You haven't known you were a brother for long, though."

His smile was grim. "I certainly haven't acknowledged it. But I am her brother, and I intend to help." His lips relaxed a little. "Besides, I've grown very attached to my niece. I hope to see a lot of Barbara and Darcy."

"That's very good news, Wyatt."

Angela pushed back her chair and stood. "I should be on my way. Thank you for the coffee and cake."

"Anytime," Elli responded, relieved that their guest was leaving. She felt as if she was playing a very bad game of charades, and that at any moment Angela Beck would see clear through both of them.

"Any idea how long Barbara will remain in hospital?" Wyatt retrieved her coat and followed her to the door, while Elli hung back at the doorway to the kitchen.

"My understanding is that the doctors are evaluating her every day. While I don't have a specific time line, I believe it will be soon." She smiled then, buttoning her coat. "Your life will be back to normal before you know it, Wyatt." She looked over his shoulder at Elli. "You, too, Ellison."

Wyatt walked her to her car while Elli went back to the kitchen to tidy the mess. Back to normal? The idea was not as grand as it might have been a week ago. Did she want her life to return to normal? Back to the Camerons', back to looking for a job and a place to live, back to a world without Wyatt in it?

She knew the answer already. A world without Wyatt was gray, rather than filled with dazzling color. Was it so wrong to hope that today meant something more? As much as she would miss Darcy, didn't an end to their foster care mean that they wouldn't have to pretend, too?

Wyatt came back inside, shutting the door quietly behind him. The nerves in Elli's tummy started twisting and turning, both in anticipation and a little afraid of what to say now that they were alone. The first private words since being seminaked with him on his bed.

"That was close."

She put down the sugar bowl and went to the arch dividing the living room and kitchen. "I'm sorry." She felt she needed to offer an apology. She should have thought more and felt less. She had let her need for him cloud her judgment and they'd nearly been caught.

"Don't be sorry. I shouldn't have taken advantage."

Her head whirled. "Advantage?"

Wyatt's jaw tightened. "You were vulnerable this morning. It wasn't fair of me to…" He swallowed, as though there were something big in his throat he was trying to get around. "To kiss you."

She wanted to say *Maybe I wanted you to,* but the words wouldn't come. Because he wasn't looking conflicted about it at all. If he had gazed at her now with some sort of longing, some sort of indication that restraint came at a cost, she might have pushed. But his back was ramrod straight, his expression closed where earlier it had been transparent. The shrinking feeling in her chest was the dwindling of hope. Hope that he'd feel about her the same way she did about him.

"I can take the chair back out," he suggested.

"No!" She straightened, took a step forward. "Please don't. It's a beautiful chair, Wyatt, and you did a lovely job refinishing it. I'll be fine now. Really."

"Are you sure?"

She nodded. "Yes, I'm sure. It was so thoughtful of you

and it will make things so comfortable. I didn't realize I'd react so strongly. But it's over now, right?" Emotional hurt became a physical pain as she lifted her chin. "Don't give this morning another thought."

"Only if you're sure, Elli."

"I'm sure."

"All right, then."

She fought against the shock rippling through her as he ended the topic of conversation. They weren't even going to talk about what had happened? What had almost happened? Did he regret it that much? The thought made her crumple inside.

He moved to the sofa and retrieved the hat he'd dropped there earlier. "I'll be out moving the herd to back pasture," he said, and without another word he left.

Elli woke, an uneasy feeling permeating her consciousness. Moonlight sent faded beams through the window blind of the bedroom, and it was utterly quiet. Too quiet, she realized. Blinking away the grit in her eyes, she slid out of bed and went to the playpen to check on Darcy.

She wasn't there.

But the bedroom door was half-open and Elli padded over to it. She opened it the rest of the way with only a small creak and tiptoed down the hall. The blanket on the sofa was crumpled in a heap and the pillow held the indentation of Wyatt's head. In the slight light of the moon, Elli saw them.

Darcy's hands peeped out from beneath her blanket and her lips were open, completely relaxed with the telltale shine of a dribble of milk trailing from the corner of her mouth to her chin. She lay ensconced in Wyatt's arms, the latter clad in only a T-shirt and navy boxer shorts. His jeans lay neatly folded across the arm of the sofa. Heat flooded her cheeks at the sight of his bare feet and long legs. His eyes were closed, but she knew he was not quite asleep. One foot flexed slightly, rocking the chair gently back and forth.

He would be such a wonderful father, she thought as she watched them. Not once in this whole ordeal had he ever put Darcy somewhere other than first. She couldn't think of one single man who would have stepped up in the same circumstances with equal dedication and without resentment. There had been moments at the beginning that they'd fumbled with knowing what to do, but he had taken it on and he'd done it out of not only obligation but love.

He had so much to give. She wondered if he realized it, or if what he'd told her about his past crippled him the way her grief had crippled her.

The toe stopped pushing against the floor and the chair stopped. Wyatt's eyes opened and met hers across the living room.

Elli struggled to breathe, suddenly feeling as if there wasn't enough air in the room to fill her lungs. She was drawn back in the flash of a moment to yesterday morning, and what it was like to be held and protected in his arms. They'd been stilted and polite since, but now with her feet bare and wearing nothing but a nightgown, she felt the awareness return, sharper and stronger than before.

In the gray light his eyes appeared darker than ever and her nerve endings seemed to stand on end. The soft curves of the rocking chair and the pink-blanketed baby were in contradiction to the ruggedness of Wyatt's body. In that moment, with his gaze locked with hers, she understood what people said about men with babies. Strength and frailty, shadow and light, toughness and tenderness. It was a combination Elli was helpless against.

"She woke up," Wyatt whispered in the dark, setting the chair in slow motion again.

Elli put one foot in front of the other and perched on the edge of the sofa, only inches from where his bare knee moved as the chair came forward. "I didn't hear her," she replied, as quietly as she could. Not only because of Darcy, but because she was afraid to break the tentative shell around them.

"You were sound asleep," Wyatt answered, and she saw the corners of his lips tip up slightly. "You never moved when I went in to get her."

Elli looked away, staring at her fingers as they rested on her knees. Wyatt had been in the bedroom, watching her sleep? It was intensely personal and she wondered what he'd thought as he'd seen her there in his bed.

She'd been exhausted tonight and had to admit that she'd had the deepest, most restful sleep in months. It didn't escape her notice that it followed the purging of her grief earlier.

"What time is it?"

"Nearly five."

Goodness, she'd gone to bed before nine. For the first time in weeks she'd had a solid eight hours of sleep.

"I'm sorry I didn't get up with her." Elli noted the empty bottle on the table. She'd slept through it all, including Wyatt heating a bottle.

"I enjoyed it," he replied, smiling. "It wasn't long ago I would have thought it crazy to say such a thing. But for someone so small, she sure has a way of making us come around, doesn't she?"

The way he said *us* sent another warm curl through Elli's insides. Right now, in the predawn hours, it could almost be easy to believe that they were a perfect little family. It felt that way—adorable child, tired mother, husband who got up instead with the baby so mom could rest.

But that wasn't reality. It was a fantasy, a life she'd wanted more than anything before having to trade in her dreams for new ones. They were only playacting. Darcy was not theirs, and Wyatt was not hers.

"Let me put her back to bed," Elli suggested. "You need your sleep. You can get a couple more hours before breakfast."

She and Wyatt stood at the same time, and Elli put her arms out for Darcy. But switching her from Wyatt's embrace to Elli's was awkward, the more so because they didn't want to wake her. Wyatt's arm brushed hers, firm and warm. As he placed Darcy in the crook of Elli's arm, his fingers brushed over her breast.

Both of them froze.

Elli bit down on her lip, realizing that she was braless and once more aware that she was clad only in a light cotton nightie that ended at her knees. And Wyatt...he was holding himself so stiffly, careful not to touch her in any way. Her teeth worried at the tender flesh of her bottom lip as she tried not to be hurt by that. He was so close she could feel the heat from his body, the soft fabric of his T-shirt. And oh, the scent of him. The faded woodsy notes of his body wash from his earlier shower, mingled with sleep.

What would happen if she moved an inch closer? Two? If she tipped up her head to ask for his kiss? Would he accept the invitation?

Or would he step back, as he had that night on the veranda, and as he had yesterday after Angela Beck's visit? She wanted to tell him how she felt, but needed some sign from him first, something to encourage her that she was not alone. And since the accidental touch, he was not moving any closer.

So she moved back, adjusting Darcy's weight. "Good night," she murmured, too late realizing how silly it sounded, since it was already nearly morning. She turned away and took Darcy to the bedroom, not looking back.

It didn't matter.

The sight of him there, standing in the dark, was already branded painfully on her brain and heart.

Exactly two weeks after Darcy had been deposited on Wyatt's veranda she went home to her mother.

Neither Elli nor Wyatt were prepared for the news; despite Angela Beck's visit they had expected temporary care to last longer as Barbara regained her feet. For Elli it was too soon and yet too long as well; she already loved Darcy and felt a bond between them. There was no question that Darcy belonged with Barbara, but it was equally true that Elli had become attached to the blue-eyed angel who had been dropped into her life unceremoniously and was now leaving it under much different circumstances.

She had her goodbye moment with Darcy as she put her down for her morning nap. She kissed the warm temple, her nostrils filled with the scent of baby lotion and sweetness. She was determined not to cry, but wiped below her eyes anyway at the bit of moisture that was there. She had a lot to thank Darcy for—she could feel in her heart that healing strides had been taken. Sadness for William now wasn't as piercing as before. Somehow between Darcy's innocence and Wyatt's gentleness she'd been able to let go of the grief that had stopped her from living.

But goodbyes of any sort hurt, and she knew she had to do it now and get it over with, so that later she could simply pick up her things and leave.

She was folding the freshly laundered sleeper sets she'd

bought and laying them in the bottom of the diaper bag when Wyatt came in.

He said nothing, just went to the change table, picked up a soft stuffed bunny and turned it over in his hands. Elli kept folding and packing until there was nothing left to fold.

She looked up at Wyatt, who was watching her with worried eyes.

"Are you okay with this?" She voiced the question that he would not.

"You mean her going back to Barbara?"

Elli nodded.

"I don't have a choice," he replied, but Elli knew he was avoiding the real answer.

"I didn't ask that. I asked how you felt about it."

It felt good, being direct with him, especially since they'd danced around any type of personal topic since Angela Beck's visit. Darcy would be leaving today. So would she. There was no more time to leave things for later.

He stopped worrying the bunny and put the toy down on the bed. "We were told it wasn't going to be long," he said. "But of course I'm worried. I'm happy Barbara's done so well and that the doctors think she's ready. But she has a long road ahead of her, especially as a single mom. It is so much for her to handle."

"Family services will still be involved."

"Yes, of course. And her doctor, too. I spoke to her doctor this morning, and there are support systems in place. It all sounds fine."

"Yet you don't sound convinced."

He looked up and met her gaze. "I worry, that's all. One thing I know for sure. Barbara will have me behind her.

I'm going to be there for her. As her brother and as Darcy's uncle. Lucky for her, now I have practice as a babysitter."

"More than a babysitter, Wyatt." Elli zipped up the bag. "A father. You have been a father to Darcy these last two weeks."

His expression was difficult to decipher. Elli saw pleasure, but also pain, and perhaps denial. Knowing what she did about him, she could understand where such emotions might come from. But he wouldn't talk to her, not anymore. Ever since that morning when Angela Beck had shown up, he'd been closed off. And any softening that had happened in the dark at 5:00 a.m. was gone now. Perhaps there had been a mutual attraction, and something more than friendship between them. But there wasn't the trust she thought. Not from Wyatt. He'd backed away and hadn't had any trouble keeping away.

She'd already been in a relationship where they hadn't talked about their true feelings, and it had been their downfall. She wouldn't do it again. So she tried to make this, the end, as amicable as possible. "You made everything right for Barbara and Darcy," she said.

"You were the one who made this work," he replied, refusing to accept her words. "You were with her day and night, caring for her, making this place a home. And you accepted nothing for it. You didn't even deposit the check I wrote you. I checked. Why?"

Because I needed you. She heard the answer inside her head, but it never reached her lips.

With that answer, she began to doubt. Were her feelings for him solely wrapped up in overcoming her own problems? The answer hadn't come to her as *I love you.* It had been about need, and grief, and moving forward. She didn't want to think she'd used him, and she certainly hadn't meant to, but there was no denying the possibility that her feelings had been influenced by her needs. And with that possibility, the seeds of doubt were planted.

"I did it because I wanted to."

Wyatt stepped forward and reached for her arm. "Not good enough."

His hand on her biceps was firm and she shook it off. "I'm sorry if you're not satisfied."

She reached for the bag she'd already packed. She couldn't wait around for Barbara to arrive, to see Darcy put in her car seat and to watch her leave, taking a piece of Elli's heart with her. She had to get out now. Just his hand on her arm created a maelstrom of emotion she didn't want to deal with. Not today. Not with everything else.

"Elli…" His voice had a strain on it she hadn't heard before. "You're leaving. Can't we be honest before you go?"

Her heart pounded, wanting to be. But over the course of the past few years, so many of the things she'd thought were true had been only illusions. Could she say for certain this wasn't the same thing?

The issue of propriety during Darcy's stay was ended as of today. And yet he hadn't once said, *Please don't go.* He'd said, *You're leaving.*

"What do you want me to say, Wyatt?" She turned around to face him, willing her voice not to quiver. "Our deal was that I would stay and help you as long as Darcy was here. But she's not going to be here any longer and I am no longer needed as your nanny. Because that's what I've been, right? Darcy's nanny."

Her fingers gripped the handle of her bag, while every pore of her wanted to hear him contradict her. Not long ago he'd said very clearly that she was more than a nanny. Had that changed? The other morning, in the dark, her invitation couldn't have been more clear, but he hadn't stepped forward and taken what was offered.

"You weren't a nanny that morning here on my bed, were you." He said it as a statement, not a question. And the snap in his voice put Elli's back up.

"You cooled off soon enough." Oh bravo, Elli, she thought, seeing Wyatt's shocked expression. He hadn't been expecting such a quick response, she could tell. He couldn't put this all on her. If she'd given mixed signals, she'd taken the lead from him.

"Angela Beck at the door put things in perspective quite quickly," he replied. His forehead seemed to flatten as if he were displeased. "Getting caught would have been a disaster. Like you said before—our relationship had to be platonic."

"I don't want to argue before I leave, Wyatt. Please, can't we just leave things on good terms? You got what you wanted all along. You got to keep Darcy and fulfill your responsibility to your family. You did the right thing. Let's just leave it at that."

"And did you get what you wanted?"

The words hurt, because he didn't know what she wanted and she was too afraid to tell him. She was too afraid to ask how he felt about her and get pushed away again. Twice had been more than enough. Every single time in her life that she'd tried to be open with her feelings she'd been shut down. And Wyatt wasn't offering her anything in return, any level of safety that if she did open up would make it worth it.

"What do you *want* out of life, Elli?"

As he said the harsh words, the planes of his face changed, more angled and taut. He ran a hand through his hair that even when messy looked as if it was that way deliberately. She wanted to throw off the cloak of all her misgivings and just tell him how she felt. But she couldn't. She could still hear Tim's words in her ears, the ones she'd passed off as coming from bitterness and pain. She understood now that there had been a kernel of truth in them just the same and that they had affected her even if she hadn't wanted them to. Words that had cut her to the quick. *Go ahead. Walk out on our marriage. You failed our baby and I'm just another casualty.*

The words came back with disturbing clarity now because she knew they were true.

She did blame herself for William's death, and she did walk out on their marriage.

CHAPTER TWELVE

WYATT WATCHED THE COLOR drain from Elli's cheeks. Her eyes loomed large within the pale skin of her face. It was a fair question. What did she want, and why wouldn't she just say it? Now that Darcy was leaving, nothing stood in their way. Why wouldn't she come to him?

He had seen her face when she'd come into the kitchen the day Angela Beck had visited. Maybe they'd both been carried away in the moment, but he hadn't expected her cool response. They'd both known what could have happened if they'd been caught together, what else could he have done? And he'd tried to bridge the gap by offering to remove the chair, but she'd stared at him with those huge eyes and he'd felt the gap between them widen.

She was afraid, and he knew it. This morning he'd tried pushing to see if he could make her react with honesty, but if anything she was withdrawing further. And he couldn't do it anymore, not knowing how fragile she was. Maybe she needed more time. He would never push where he wasn't wanted; he'd seen his father muscle his way through relationships enough to know making demands and bullying didn't work. You couldn't force love. And he was pretty sure he was falling in love with Elli.

What would she do if he just came right out and said it?

As they stared at each other, her chalk-white and him

with tension cording every muscle, he knew exactly what she'd do. She'd run.

"I've got to go."

"Elli." He took a step forward, and in spite of his determination not to push he found himself gripping the tops of her arms, forcing her to look up at him, wanting to grab one last chance. "Don't run."

The color rushed back into her cheeks and her blue gaze snapped up at him. "What are you offering, Wyatt? What do *you* want out of life? Because knowing that would help me out a lot. I can't figure you out, I really can't. And the last week and a half, you've gone out of your way to stay out of *my* way."

His hands felt burned and he dropped them away from her arms. Is that what she thought? That he couldn't stand to be near her? "Me?"

"You were the one that set up boundaries!" she cried.

Their gazes clashed and his dropped to her lips briefly, watching them open as her breaths seemed to accelerate.

"To protect Darcy!" Frustration was suddenly added to the cocktail of feelings rushing through him.

"Only Darcy?"

She'd very effectively turned the tables on him and he felt a slide of guilt run up his spine. All right, so maybe he was being cautious. And maybe he'd used Darcy as a shield to keep from admitting how he really felt. But he kept quiet now because he wasn't sure of her. He'd been there when she'd fallen apart and he'd seen her withdraw into herself afterward. She wasn't ready. He knew she was afraid. What woman wouldn't be after what she'd been through? He couldn't force her to open up.

"Fine. You want to know what I want, Elli? I'll tell you. I want this ranch to prosper, I want this house a home, I want a wife to love and a couple of kids. I want the kind of marriage my mother and father never had and I want to provide my children with the childhood *I* never had. I want the past to stop defining me and I want to prove that a pattern doesn't have to be continued." It all came out in a rush and it felt damn good to say it.

"Now go ahead." He lowered his voice and looked down at her, knowing she hadn't expected such an outburst. "Run. I know that's what you want to do."

She hadn't moved a muscle, but it seemed suddenly as if an invisible wall rose between them. Her complete withdrawal was cool and palpable. This was why he'd resisted. Because he'd known exactly how she'd react.

"I have to go," she whispered.

Her response didn't surprise him, but he felt the dull ache of disappointment. He couldn't beg for someone to love him. He'd left that little boy behind him long ago and he had too much pride. He went to the end of the bed, picked up the bag she had dropped when he'd grabbed her arms. "I'll walk you out."

Silently they went to the front door and Wyatt opened it. The fall air had a bite to it; in the low places of the yard the grass was still silvery with frost. Sunlight glinted off the few golden leaves remaining on the border of aspens. It was a perfect fall day. And yet there was no joy in it for Wyatt. By tonight he would be alone in his house again, only this time he'd feel the solitude much more keenly.

They hesitated on the porch for only a moment. Wyatt held out her bag and Elli took it without meeting his eyes. "Thank you for everything," he said, knowing it sounded formal, but pride kept him from speaking more intimately. "If there's ever anything you need…"

"Don't," she commanded softly. "Please, not this cold politeness. Not after everything."

She walked down the steps and half turned, and he

thought he caught a glimpse of moisture in her eyes before she blinked and it was gone.

"Goodbye, Wyatt."

He waited on the porch, watching her walk away down the dirt drive, feeling his heart go with her. Wishing she'd turn around and come back, hoping she'd be as honest with him as he'd been with her. If she would only do that, they might stand a chance. He needed her to stop. To come back to him. To let him make everything right somehow.

But she didn't. She walked on, her strides never faltering.

And as she reached his mailbox, a car slowed and made the turn into his driveway.

Barbara was here.

Elli felt every pound of her bag as the strap dug into her shoulder. She wouldn't look back. She couldn't. If she did, her resolve would falter. No, she reminded herself, holding the strap for dear life, she had to be strong. This time she had to be strong. This time she had to see the reality, not the dream. And the reality was Wyatt didn't love her, not the way she needed him to. Not the way she loved him.

As she stepped onto the interlocking blocks of the Camerons' front walk, she couldn't help but look over toward the house. A woman—dark hair, tall, like Wyatt—got out of the car, and Elli paused. It was like watching an accident and being unable to turn away even though she knew she should. Wyatt went down the steps with Darcy bundled in her blanket. Across the two lawns she heard Barbara's exclamation and saw her take the baby from Wyatt's arms. The way she held her, close to her body and with her head dropped low, made Elli's eyes sting. Barbara rocked Darcy in her arms even though she was standing, and Elli saw her kiss the perfectly shaped forehead.

She couldn't watch anymore.

Numbly she unlocked the door and stepped inside. She'd once been awed by the foyer's perfection, its opulence. Now it felt cold and empty. The cavernous foyer echoed with the closing of the door. She trudged up the tile steps to the living room, stared out the huge windows at the prairie extended before her, so vast and unforgiving. She took her bag to the guest room, dropped it inside and waited. For a sound. For anything.

But nothing came.

Next door, Wyatt was reconnecting with his sister and reconciling his past. Darcy would be going home, but he would see her often. She imagined them sitting in his kitchen now, perhaps drinking coffee, laughing, talking. He hadn't had to say goodbye to Darcy, as well. But she had lost both of them. She was alone.

And the worst part of it was that she knew she'd brought it on herself.

She'd said yes to his plea for help. She'd gone and fallen for him despite all her self-warnings to stay detached. And in the end she'd been too afraid to tell him how she felt, and so here she was. Alone. Again.

She told herself it didn't matter, because her feelings weren't returned anyway. She told herself it was better this way, because it wouldn't be right to stay so attached to him, or to his niece. She couldn't leave Darcy out of this either; she loved her, too, and felt the loss of her deep inside. And in that moment Elli realized an important truth. She was a mother. Maybe she hadn't had the opportunity to watch William grow, but she had loved him. She had a mother's heart.

Bereft, she buried her face in the pillow and let out the tears she'd held in all morning.

* * *

With a broad smile Wyatt refilled their soup bowls and sat back down at the table. He wasn't much of a cook, not like Elli. He missed her smiles already. He pushed the thoughts aside, to bring out later when he was alone. Tonight marked a milestone, even if his best efforts managed only canned soup and a sandwich. Reuniting with his sister seemed to eclipse his lack of culinary expertise.

"Sorry it's not fancier."

"Don't be silly." Barbara picked up her spoon and smiled. "Thank you. One of the things I promised the doctor I'd do for myself was eat better. This is just what I needed."

"Are you really okay?" Wyatt halted the progress of his spoon and his smile faded a bit. "I mean, you're going to be back to caring for Darcy full-time again. You're sure you're ready?"

Barbara's smile faded as the mood turned sober. "I'd be a liar if I said I wasn't scared. But I'm learning coping skills and I have a number to call anytime, day or night. Don't worry, Wyatt. Everyone is following up on me."

"That day or night thing," he said, putting down his spoon and taking her hand. "That goes for me, too. I suspected about our father all along, but I was a coward and said nothing. But not anymore. I'd like to be your brother, if you want me to."

Tears filled Barbara's eyes and she squeezed his hand. "You always were a good kid, and you turned into a good man. Even when I wasn't thinking clearly, I know I wouldn't have trusted you with Darcy if I hadn't believed you'd do your best by her. You went home with a black eye because of me once, Wyatt. I haven't forgotten."

"It's good to have family again," he said simply.

"Yes, it is. And I know you had help. Where's Ellison?"

Wyatt suddenly became engrossed with his soup bowl,

feeling pain at even the mention of her name and not wanting to show it to Barbara. "She's gone home."

"I want to thank her for all she's done."

Of course she did, Wyatt realized. But not now. "Now is probably not a good time, Barb. I think it was very difficult for her to leave Darcy."

He felt Barb's eyes assessing and stood up, taking his bowl to the sink.

"Only Darcy?"

A heaviness settled in his heart. "I don't know." He braced his hands on the edge of the counter.

"Is there something between you two?"

Wyatt turned around. Maybe he and Barb had a lot of missing gaps, but she had known him a long time, since they were children and in school together.

"Even if there was, there isn't now."

"I'm sorry, Wyatt. Are you in love with her?"

He had known his father's cruelty, but she had known his neglect. Now she was dealing with the results of her own failed relationship and making her way as a single parent. The way she was looking at him now told him she understood a little of what he was fighting against.

"I am."

"So what's stopping you from fighting for her?"

"We're not the only ones damaged here, Barb. Elli's had her own troubles to deal with. I got to a point where I was ready to move past it and take the life I wanted. But she's not there yet. And I can't do it for her."

Darcy made happy-baby noises from her seat and Barbara smiled. "I should get her home."

She rose and went to the seat, buckling Darcy in and picking up a blanket to lay over her.

"You'll be okay?"

"I'll be fine."

"You'll call me tomorrow?"

Barbara smiled. "You getting all big brother on me now?"

Wyatt grinned. "Feels weird, huh? But yeah, I guess I am."

To his surprise, Barbara came to him and hugged him. "Thank you," she murmured, and backed off slightly. "Sometimes the worst part in all of this is feeling alone. I think I'll like having a big brother."

He walked her out, taking the bag of clothes while she carried the seat. As they secured Darcy in the backseat, he added, "I kept the playpen and change table. Any time you need a break, Darcy's welcome to come stay with Uncle Wyatt."

"Thank you."

As Barbara started the engine and backed out of the driveway, Wyatt stood and lifted his hand in farewell.

When she was gone he went back inside, but the house felt instantly different. Empty, and lifeless. For two weeks it had been filled with noise and discord, but also with happy moments and somehow, family. Darcy had gone home with her mother, but he would see her again. He was her uncle. But Elli—soon she'd be leaving and heading off to wherever life was going to take her. And he missed her most of all. The way she looked sitting across from him at the table, or the way she joked with him about his sweet tooth. How she looked cradling Darcy in her arms, giving her a bottle, and how sweet she tasted when he kissed her.

He stared out the kitchen window, looking over the dark fields. They undulated like inky-black curves as cloud covered the rising moon. Droplets of rain began to splash against the pane, suiting his mood. He had tried to tell her what he wanted earlier today and she had been too afraid to reach out and grab it. He knew he couldn't force her to change.

But he also knew he didn't want to give up.

She was still at the Camerons', and he was here. Both of them alone. It didn't make sense, not when he wanted to be with her so much.

Energized, he went to the door and pulled on his boots, followed by his oilskin. All the things he should have said this morning he'd say tonight. It didn't have to be too late. He opened the door and was flipping up his collar when he saw her.

Standing at the bottom of his steps, her hair in strings from the rain, her shoulders huddled in her jacket.

For a split second they both hesitated, stared. Then he took one step outside and held out his hand.

She came up the steps and took it, her fingers ice-cold as his wrapped around them. Without saying a word, he pulled her into the circle of his arms.

They stood that way a long time, with the rhythmic patter of the rain falling on the roof of the veranda and the door wide-open behind him. Finally he kissed the top of her head, the scent of vanilla and citrus filling his nostrils.

"Come inside," he murmured, and he drew her in out of the cold and damp.

Once inside he could see the evidence of hard crying in her pink face and puffy eyes. It gave him hope. She'd been so contained, so cold today he'd had moments wondering if maybe he had imagined their connection. And then there was Darcy to consider. He knew part of the reason she'd left first was so that she wouldn't have to watch Darcy go.

"Darcy's gone home with Barb," he said, watching, gauging her reaction.

"I know."

"The house seems empty without her."

"I know."

She said it so sadly he wondered if that was the cause of her distress, and not him at all.

"Where were you going just now?" She tilted up her face, droplets of rain clinging to her pink cheeks.

"I was coming for you."

The world opened up for Elli as he said it. Her heart, so withered and afraid, expanded, warm and beautiful. She had been coming for him, too. But hearing him say it, seeing the agony etched on his face, gave her a rush of hope.

Her bottom lip quivered with emotion and she reached out for him. Her hands spanned his ribs through the heavy jacket and he threaded his fingers through her hair. Firm hands tilted her face until she was forced to meet his gaze.

"I was coming for you," he repeated, and then he kissed her.

When he finally released her, she admitted, "I was coming for you, too."

Elli had spent hours crying and hurting, but at the end of it there had been no solution. The pain of letting go of Darcy was what she'd dreaded, but in the end it wasn't the loss of Darcy that cut deepest. It was Wyatt. She didn't want to be held prisoner by fear anymore. She'd known that even if it never worked out, she had to make the important step of telling the truth. She would never know unless she asked. His welcome was more than she had dared hope for.

"Wyatt, I…I want to answer what you asked me this morning."

They were still standing next to the front door, water dripping from their coats, but Elli didn't care.

"Okay."

"You asked me what I wanted," she began, tucking the

wet strands of her hair behind her ears. "And my answer is the same as yours. It's all I've ever wanted, my whole life. I was always a puzzle to my mom, and my friends, and then my coworkers. I didn't have lofty aspirations like they did. I didn't want to be a lawyer or a doctor or a model, or even rich. All I wanted was a home, with a husband to love and a couple of kids. I wanted the kind of marriage my mother and father had and I wanted to be a mother more than anything. And for a while I had all that, or very nearly. And it all went up in smoke. And now, finally, I know why."

"Elli, I'm so sorry about that—"

"No." Elli cut him off. "I want the past to stop defining me and I want to prove that a pattern doesn't have to be continued, just like you. I'm done with settling, Wyatt. I convinced myself I could have it all with Tim, and I was wrong. I know I was wrong because..."

The next part was the hardest. It was putting herself out there, being emotionally naked. But what was the alternative? What more did she have to lose? Nothing. This afternoon had shown her that. She had cried and felt a bleakness unlike anything she'd felt before, even in her grief about William. Today she had, for a moment, given up hope, and the emptiness was more than she could bear.

"I know I was wrong because I didn't really love him. I loved the idea of him, I loved the fantasy of the perfect life I could have with him. I thought we would have it all. But it turned out it was nothing. Because I know now what it is to really love someone. The way I've fallen in love with you."

Her voice faltered to a near whisper as she finished, trying desperately not to cry, trying to fight back the fear she felt in admitting such a thing. Wyatt was gaping at her, saying nothing, his face a mask of surprise. And well he should be surprised. After holding things so tightly in her heart, letting them out in such a rush was unexpected.

"I gave up last time without a fight. Maybe because it wasn't worth fighting for. But you are, Wyatt. I don't want to walk away from you. I want those things with you. Is there a chance you might want them with me, too?"

She stood back, chin quivering, waiting for his answer.

He exhaled, the sound an emotional choke as he stepped forward. "Look at you—you're soaked."

She let him unzip her jacket and slide it down her shoulders. It dropped to the floor in a damp puddle. He cupped her jaw in his hands and forced her to look into his eyes.

"I love you, Elli."

He dipped his head and kissed her, the sweetest thing she had ever known. "It took you long enough," he murmured against her lips, and then he wrapped his arms around her ribs and lifted her off her feet. "I told myself I had to wait for you to be ready. But tonight, alone...I just couldn't."

She nuzzled against the collar of his jacket, smelling the unique scent of leather and rain and man mixed together. Joy rushed through her, chasing away the fear. Wyatt wouldn't say it unless he meant it. He loved her. She closed her eyes. She could handle anything if he truly loved her.

A laugh bubbled past her lips. "Long enough? We've only known each other a few weeks."

He only squeezed tighter. "We spent more time together the last two weeks than most people do dating. We shared things, things I hadn't told another person. What does time matter, anyway? I knew the night on the porch when we kissed."

"Then? When you pushed me away and decreed our relationship had to be platonic?"

"Yes, back then."

She laughed again. "You were faster than me. I couldn't admit it to myself until I saw you in the rocking chair with Darcy." Tenderness overcame her. "Loving you meant facing a lot of things I was trying not to face, you know."

He finally eased his hold on her and drew back. "There's so much I want to tell you. I don't know where to start. About Barbara today, and about me, and my plans…"

His dark eyes glittered with excitement and Elli felt uplifted by the possibilities. "One thing at a time," she teased.

"Come here," he said. He shed his jacket, hung it on the hook and took her hand, leading her to the rocking chair. This silly chair, responsible for so many things, shaped and polished by his hands. Hands that were capable of so much. As he sat and pulled her onto his lap, she lifted his hands to her lips and kissed them.

"I was so scared to come here, afraid you didn't really feel the same."

"I'm glad you did," he replied, turning his hands over so he could grip hers and mimic her action. "I wasn't sure how I was going to manage without you."

"Me?" She looked at him, surprised. "Are you kidding? Look at this chair, the porch, the door. All the improvements you've made around here. Is there anything you can't do, Wyatt? That's one of the things I noticed right off. You're so very handy."

"I had to be, growing up. God knows my dad was never around. I looked after my mom."

"Like you're looking after Barbara?"

The easy expression on his face faltered a little. "I suppose. I felt like I let her down."

"Why?"

The hesitation lasted only a moment. "Because my parents only got married because my mom was pregnant with me. And my father never let me forget that he was stuck in that marriage because I'd been born. When things went badly, he made sure I knew it was all my fault."

"Oh, Wyatt, that's a horrible thing to say to a child!" Suddenly pieces began to fit. "So you take on responsibility for everyone?" Her stomach began to twist. "For me?"

He closed his eyes. "Maybe at first. Maybe I did, because I could see you were broken and I wanted to fix things for you. I tried for a long time to make things okay for my mom, even though she kept telling me it wasn't my responsibility. But this morning I knew I couldn't. I couldn't fix you. That's something you have to do for yourself. It killed me watching you walk away. But I kept thinking that if I pushed, if I didn't give you that chance, some day you'd blame me, too. And it would be too hard to truly have you and then watch you walk away."

Elli leaned back against his chest. "It wasn't until this afternoon when you weren't there anymore that I realized. Being without you made it very clear how much I love you. I couldn't picture going on without you. I knew I had to try."

"I was looking out the window thinking what a fool I'd been to let you get away. I was going over to ask you to give us a chance."

"I left because you said you wanted those things but you never said you wanted them with me."

He sighed, putting his chin on the top of her head. "And I didn't say it because I was afraid of scaring you away completely."

"We're idiots," she decreed, and felt him smile against her hair.

"No, we're not. Because we both came to our senses."

For several minutes they rocked in the chair, absorbing each other, forging a new bond, two parts of a bigger whole.

"What now?" Elli finally asked. She wanted him to ask her to come back so they could work on their relationship. What she didn't expect was what he said next.

"How do you feel about ranching, and this house?"

She sat up a bit so she could turn her head and look him square in the face. "It's very cozy here."

"Could you be a rancher's wife? I'm no doctor, and I know we had very different upbringings."

Could she! "What difference does that make? What does it matter what you do?" She touched his cheek. "I just need to be where you are. I love it here. I've felt more at home in this house than any place I can remember. It doesn't pretend to be something it's not."

"And children? I understand that's a touchy subject. Are you okay physically? God, I never even asked that before. And I get you must be scared…"

Having children *was* a scary idea, only because she knew what it was to love so deeply and lose. But the dream had just been traded in—it hadn't died. She still wanted to be a mother, more than anything. "Nothing comes without risk," she said quietly. "And the idea of babies…oh, Wyatt," she whispered, and the back of her nose stung. "Not just babies. Your babies."

She couldn't say any more. Instead, they let the idea flower, fragile and tender.

"Whatever happens, we'll weather it," he said in response.

"I know," she replied. And she did know. This was what the real deal felt like.

"I love you, Elli."

He looked up at her, his brown eyes so incredibly earnest

and that little piece of hair flopping over his forehead. She reached out and smoothed it away.

He grabbed her finger and kissed it. "Marry me?"

"In a heartbeat," she replied, and she knew what it was to be home at last.

MILLS & BOON

ROMANCE

The Reluctant Surrender	Penny Jordan
Shameful Secret, Shotgun Wedding	Sharon Kendrick
The Virgin's Choice	Jennie Lucas
Scandal: Unclaimed Love-Child	Melanie Milburne
Powerful Greek, Housekeeper Wife	Robyn Donald
Hired by Her Husband	Anne McAllister
Snowbound Seduction	Helen Brooks
A Mistake, A Prince and A Pregnancy	Maisey Yates
Champagne with a Celebrity	Kate Hardy
When He was Bad...	Anne Oliver
Accidentally Pregnant!	Rebecca Winters
Star-Crossed Sweethearts	Jackie Braun
A Miracle for His Secret Son	Barbara Hannay
Proud Rancher, Precious Bundle	Donna Alward
Cowgirl Makes Three	Myrna Mackenzie
Secret Prince, Instant Daddy!	Raye Morgan
Officer, Surgeon...Gentleman!	Janice Lynn
Midwife in the Family Way	Fiona McArthur

HISTORICAL

Innocent Courtesan to Adventurer's Bride	Louise Allen
Disgrace and Desire	Sarah Mallory
The Viking's Captive Princess	Michelle Styles

MEDICAL™

Bachelor of the Baby Ward	Meredith Webber
Fairytale on the Children's Ward	Meredith Webber
Playboy Under the Mistletoe	Joanna Neil
Their Marriage Miracle	Sue MacKay

0910 Gen Std LP

MILLS & BOON

OCTOBER 2010 LARGE PRINT TITLES

ROMANCE

Marriage: To Claim His Twins	Penny Jordan
The Royal Baby Revelation	Sharon Kendrick
Under the Spaniard's Lock and Key	Kim Lawrence
Sweet Surrender with the Millionaire	Helen Brooks
Miracle for the Girl Next Door	Rebecca Winters
Mother of the Bride	Caroline Anderson
What's A Housekeeper To Do?	Jennie Adams
Tipping the Waitress with Diamonds	Nina Harrington

HISTORICAL

Practical Widow to Passionate Mistress	Louise Allen
Major Westhaven's Unwilling Ward	Emily Bascom
Her Banished Lord	Carol Townend

MEDICAL™

The Nurse's Brooding Boss	Laura Iding
Emergency Doctor and Cinderella	Melanie Milburne
City Surgeon, Small Town Miracle	Marion Lennox
Bachelor Dad, Girl Next Door	Sharon Archer
A Baby for the Flying Doctor	Lucy Clark
Nurse, Nanny...Bride!	Alison Roberts

MILLS & BOON

NOVEMBER 2010 HARDBACK TITLES

ROMANCE

The Dutiful Wife	Penny Jordan
His Christmas Virgin	Carole Mortimer
Public Marriage, Private Secrets	Helen Bianchin
Forbidden or For Bedding?	Julia James
The Twelve Nights of Christmas	Sarah Morgan
In Christofides' Keeping	Abby Green
The Italian's Blushing Gardener	Christina Hollis
The Socialite and the Cattle King	Lindsay Armstrong
Tabloid Affair, Secretly Pregnant!	Mira Lyn Kelly
Maharaja's Mistress	Susan Stephens
Christmas with her Boss	Marion Lennox
Firefighter's Doorstep Baby	Barbara McMahon
Daddy by Christmas	Patricia Thayer
Christmas Magic on the Mountain	Melissa McClone
A FAIRYTALE CHRISTMAS	Susan Meier & Barbara Wallace
The Soldier's Untamed Heart	Nikki Logan
Dr Zinetti's Snowkissed Bride	Sarah Morgan
The Christmas Baby Bump	Lynne Marshall

HISTORICAL

Courting Miss Vallois	Gail Whitiker
Reprobate Lord, Runaway Lady	Isabelle Goddard
The Bride Wore Scandal	Helen Dickson

MEDICAL™

Christmas in Bluebell Cove	Abigail Gordon
The Village Nurse's Happy-Ever-After	Abigail Gordon
The Most Magical Gift of All	Fiona Lowe
Christmas Miracle: A Family	Dianne Drake

NOVEMBER 2010 LARGE PRINT TITLES

ROMANCE

A Night, A Secret...A Child	Miranda Lee
His Untamed Innocent	Sara Craven
The Greek's Pregnant Lover	Lucy Monroe
The Mélendez Forgotten Marriage	Melanie Milburne
Australia's Most Eligible Bachelor	Margaret Way
The Bridesmaid's Secret	Fiona Harper
Cinderella: Hired by the Prince	Marion Lennox
The Sheikh's Destiny	Melissa James

HISTORICAL

The Earl's Runaway Bride	Sarah Mallory
The Wayward Debutante	Sarah Elliott
The Laird's Captive Wife	Joanna Fulford

MEDICAL™

The Surgeon's Miracle	Caroline Anderson
Dr Di Angelo's Baby Bombshell	Janice Lynn
Newborn Needs a Dad	Dianne Drake
His Motherless Little Twins	Dianne Drake
Wedding Bells for the Village Nurse	Abigail Gordon
Her Long-Lost Husband	Josie Metcalfe